Rural Delivery

BY
G.D. PERKINS

authorHOUSE®

AuthorHouse™
1663 Liberty Drive, Suite 200
Bloomington, IN 47403
www.authorhouse.com
Phone: 1-800-839-8640

This book is a work of fiction. People, places, events, and situations are the product of the author's imagination. Any resemblance to actual persons, living or dead, or historical events, is purely coincidental.

© 2008 G.D. Perkins. All rights reserved.

No part of this book may be reproduced, stored in a retrieval system, or transmitted by any means without the written permission of the author.

First published by AuthorHouse
9/30/2008

ISBN: 978-1-4343-9702-7 (sc)
ISBN: 978-1-4343-9770-6 (hc)
Library of Congress Control Number: 2008906175

Printed in the United States of America
Bloomington, Indiana

This book is printed on acid-free paper.

COVER DESIGN BY:
GARY PERKINS

COVER ART AND
ILLUSTRATION BY:

SHARON GRAHAM
TROUT RUN GALLERY
PORT WING, WI 54865

EDITING AND
ILLUSTRATION ALIGNMENT:
ANN CLEARY

COPY EDITING:
KERRY-JO JOHNSON
LAURIE PERKINS

THIS ONE IS FOR LAURIE.

YOU ARE EVERYTHING I WISH I COULD BE.

TABLE OF CONTENTS

THE ROSE 1
NAKED FAT MAN WITH A GUN 5
SHOW DOGS 13
ROCKY'S DREAM 17
COORS….HERE'S TO YA! 21
SUP DOG 23
THE RIGHT DIRECTION 29
TANGO LIMA 33
FLYING IN FORMATION 37
PORKER 41
PLAY BALL! 45
THE WARRIOR 49
WHERE ARE THE HEROES? 51
ROLE MODEL 55
LUTEFISK SEASON 59
NO MORE YESTERDAYS 63
BUTTER PECAN 69
THE BAGPIPER AND THE GUNS 73
AT THE HOP……AT 60! 77
ME AND MY SHADOW 83
GOD'S HERE 87
A GREAT DAY FOR GOLF? 91
GREATER PORT WING OPEN 97
THE OLD MAN AND ME 103
AN EMOTIONAL DAY 107
MICE! 111
WASHIN' TRUCKS AT THE FIRE HALL 119
HOWARD AND HIS CHICKENS 125

THE LADIES OF THE SOUTH SHORE 129
SWENSON'S WIGWAM HOTEL 131
GERT DIAMON 139
THE PRETTY PONY 147
NEVER…NEVER…NEVER GIVE UP! 151
THE EULOGY 157
25 IN A ROW 161
GOING HOME 165
THE FINAL WORD 171

Good day to you!

First of all, thank you for honoring us by taking the time to pick up this book and ruffle through the first few pages.

We feel privileged that you would share your time with us in this fast-paced world.

If I may, I'd like to suggest that you take a moment to read one of the stories in "Rural Delivery."

The stories are short and there is only a limited number contained in this publication.

It was designed in that manner in order to make it your travel companion, a quick read that, hopefully, will become your friend on a commuter train into the city, a flight across our beautiful country, or a road trip in the family sedan.

The intent of these stories is to make you laugh and cry, to think about similar stories that have happened in your life, but most importantly, to leave you with a warm feeling.

We want to reach in and touch your heart.

If you like the stories, and we surely hope you do, please pass along the book to a friend after you have turned the final page.

We're more focused on the number of people reading the stories than we are on book sales.

The title of this book, "Rural Delivery," seemed appropriate as we were pecking away at the keyboard in our studio at Port Wing, a tiny village of some 500 people on the shore of Lake Superior, in northwestern Wisconsin.

I think a goodly number of writers use that snooty term, "studio," when they talk about the secluded place of inspiration for their work.

Actually, our "studio" is a room over the garage, so most of these stories were written over the trucks and other junk as I inhaled gasoline fumes and looked out over an empty field and Barney's barn across the road.

I wouldn't have it any other way.

I love the peaceful view.

We're privileged to live in this small town.

As I often say, Ozzie and Harriet still live in Port Wing, and we're lucky enough to be their neighbors.

We're small town people and proud of it!

Several of our friends and neighbors were instrumental in putting together the layout for this book.

Sharon Graham was kind enough to help us with the cover art and illustrations.

She has the ice cream shop and Trout Run Art Gallery, just up the street from our studio.

That ice cream shop has been responsible for several of the too many pounds I carry on this massive frame.

Whenever I need an opinion on a story, I stop by to see Claudette, Connie, and Laverne at the bank.

They're next door to Trout Run, so it's also a good reason to stop by for an ice cream cone.

Cookie dough is my personal favorite....triple scoop.

We always get positive input on our stories from the folks at the bank, but I think they may be influenced by my wife, who frequently stops by with still warm from the oven chocolate chip cookies.

Small town America.

I love it!

By the way, the two dogs on the cover of the book are Rocky and Rose.

They came into our life after we lost our dear friend, Ashley Rose, several years ago.

I think most of us, at some point in our life, have had a companion like Ashley Rose...or Rocky....or Rose.

It may have been a dog, a cat, a gerbil or even a goldfish.

It doesn't matter, these special creatures leave us with good memories, and that's what we need every day as we continue our journey through life.

With that in mind, it seems only appropriate that we begin our series of stories with some of the good memories that have been generated for our family by Ashley Rose....Rocky and Rose.

It makes me feel good just to see their names.

So....let's turn the page and take a look at the package that comes to you via "Rural Delivery."

Ashley Rose
1989 - 2000

If tears would build a staircase . . .
we would climb right up to heaven
and bring you back home.

Author Unknown

THE ROSE

Ashley Rose died in the spring of 2000.

It was one of those dreary days in March, when grey skies and raindrops reflect your pain.

My wife, Laurie, was with Rose when she died.

She held her for the longest time, then quietly stroked her back and looked into her eyes until our dear friend slipped away in the early evening.

Laurie's strength on this day was remarkable and inspiring.

I was in Arizona, which was just as well.

I don't think I could have been there when Rose left us.

It is painful, even after all these years, to think back on that day.

Quite frankly, there are tears splattering the keyboard as these words are written.

We loved her without reservation, and that love was returned.

She was eleven years old when she died.

Our hearts were broken then and still are today.

It was her time, she was in pain, but it is so hard to let go.

Ashley Rose was a beautiful Shitz Tzu.

We brought her ashes home and swore we would never have another dog.

She arrived at our house on Mother's Day, 1989, when our daughters brought home a bundle of fur from down the block.

They made a collective plea to the old man: "We want to buy this for Mom. It's our Mother's Day present."

Between the three of them, they may have raised, in total, a few cents short of a dollar, so they wanted Dad to buy the little fur ball for Mom.

I took a very strong position.

"Absolutely not, under any circumstances, will we have a dog in the house!"

Later that day, when the dog was delivered, I slapped leather for $300 and the girls gave Mom her Mother's Day gift.

Mom was delighted!

We named her Ashley Rose, but we called her "The Rose."

She was a beautiful friend and companion.

We adored her, and she returned the favor, to all of us, even the guy who didn't want a dog.

Rose comforted Heather when she was diagnosed with diabetes, she watched the girls graduate from high school, then college.

She welcomed grandchildren and calmed us all at some point in her life.

If I or one of the girls was sick, Rose would be in bed with us until we got better.

When Laurie was sick, Rose got sick too.

Her evenings were spent on Laurie's lap, quietly napping, while Laurie read or watched television.

For many years, Laurie and Rose were masters of synchronized snoring, with one inhaling while the other exhaled.

Laurie never believed me, until I recorded the event one evening, but that's a story for another time.

As she got older, Rose began to have health problems, just annoying little matters that seemed to build upon themselves, until that dreary March afternoon when the pain became too much and she slipped away.

I hope dogs go to heaven, because I plan to be there and I want to see "The Rose" again.

Never again, Laurie and I both agreed, never…. never again, will we have a dog.

There could never be another dog that we love as much as "The Rose."

We did very well on that promise for several years, but then I began noticing hints from Laurie that maybe she would like to have another dog.

I suppose she came to that conclusion because I chase her around the house and she feeds me, then cleans up after me.

Might as well have something smaller that can sit on your lap.

Again, I took a strong position and said: "Absolutely not, under any circumstances, will we have a dog in the house."

A few weeks later, Rock and Rose were face down in their dinner dish in our kitchen.

As you can see, I maintained my strong position. We don't have a dog in the house….we have two.

Rock and Rose are two years old now.

Some days they drive us crazy, but it's a nice type of insanity.

All too often, I watch them scrambling around the house and reflect on how much they have the mannerisms of Ashley Rose.

Now, Laurie has two dogs sitting on her lap in the evening and two dogs who get sick when she gets sick.

They never leave her side.

What marvelous devotion.

Rose has the dazzling personality.

Just this past week, Laurie had their breakfast ready, but had to go to her upstairs office to send a fax.

She left their dishes setting on the kitchen counter.

I heard Rose squeaking downstairs, but then it got quiet.

A few seconds later, there's a thump on the bed and Rose has her nose an inch from mine.

She cranked up her paw, gave me a solid shot to the chops, jumped off the bed and stood by the door, looking over her shoulder, expecting me to get moving.

We went downstairs, where I found Rose standing at the counter, looking up at the breakfast dishes, then back at me.

I could feel her thinking: "What's the problem? It's ready, get it down here!"

Rock was sitting in a leather chair, letting Rose handle the conflict resolution.

They do drive you crazy sometimes, but, as said earlier, it's a nice insanity.

I know I shouldn't, but every now and then I think of the day when these beautiful creatures will leave us and it breaks my heart.

To counter that, I make it a point to let them know every day how much they're loved.

Wouldn't it be nice if we made it a point to include a similar gesture to all creatures that touch our lives every day, including the humans?

Naked Fat Man with a Gun

NAKED FAT MAN WITH A GUN

I must preface this story with a caveat.

I have been lucky enough to be married to my wife, Laurie, for more than 22 years.

During that time, I have never seen her panic.

She has always faced any emergency situation with a calm, logical, demeanor, without becoming hysterical.

There have been a number of these situations in our marriage over the past two decades, always handled in the same manner....emotions under control, problem addressed calmly.

That being said, I take you to a quiet Sunday morning, Father's Day in Port Wing.

It's a beautiful day.

Laurie had gotten up earlier, leaving me upstairs to take a shower and get ready for the day.

I had just limped out of the shower, made a few comments about my weight, covered the mirror and began toweling off.

From downstairs, I hear a totally hysterical woman screaming,

"HELP ME.....HELP ME.

PLEASE HURRY!

I NEED YOU.......I NEED HELP....PLEASE HURRY.

HELP ME!!!!

OMIGOD.....HELP ME......HURRY!!!!!!!!!"

My immediate thought is someone, or something, is attacking Laurie..... right in our own home!

I drop the towel, grab a large caliber pistol, and charge downstairs to save my wife.

Now, let's pause a moment here so you can get the picture.

Here's what we have....a naked fat man, with a gun, charging down the stairs at what must be considered full speed for a man his age.

The fat cat charges into the den, pistol at the ready.

There's no one there.

Front porch....no one there.

"WHERE ARE YOU?"

That seemed to be a logical question at the time.

It's answered by another scream.

"PLEASE HELP.....PLEASE HELP.....OMIGOD....I CAN'T STOP IT!"

The sweat is starting to bead up on the naked body now.

This is serious.

No time to call 911.

Gotta handle this one myself.

Dining room, which incidentally, is all windows.

No one there.

Another scream.

"WHY AREN'T YOU HELPING ME??? I'M ALL BLOODY!"

That brings my heart into my mouth.

I finally realize the voice is coming from the back of the house, so I adjust my focus and charge toward the assault.

"I'M ON THE WAY BABY. HANG IN THERE!!"

I'm ready to make this dog hunt!

Pistol in hand, I kick open the back door, afraid of what I'm going to see, but ready to handle the situation.

As soon as I kick open the door, one of our new puppies comes charging across the deck at a full gallop, zooms between my legs, and dives into his kennel.

As I'm turning to look at the hightailin' dog, the door slams shut on my bare foot.

The blood is flowing freely from my injured foot, while the dog is whimpering behind me in the kennel.

Now I'm screaming, naked, on the deck, with a pistol, dancing on one leg.

Can you picture this whole scenario?

"STOP......STOP......STOP.......PLEEEEEEEEEEEASE STOP!!"

Laurie's scream snaps me back to the emergency.

I recognize Laurie's scream is coming from the sauna.

I charge across the back deck, naked, a knight on a white horse, so to speak, ready to save the damsel in distress.

Standing in front of the sauna door with the pistol in the ready position, I kick the sauna door with my good foot.

It doesn't budge, but I thought I heard a bone crack.

I kick it again.

It doesn't budge, probably because I slipped this time on the blood pouring from my other foot.

Now let's pause a moment to picture this scenario.

Fat guy, naked, foot bleeding, with a gun, in full view of the neighbors, kicking a door.

Uh Huh.

As I'm winding up to kick the door again, Laurie opens it and peeks around the corner.

I'm already into the kick, so there's no resistance when the door opens.

I go flying into the sauna, slip on the floor, and fall on my hip.

Not only did I pull a hamstring, I'm thinking I cracked a hipbone.

No time for that.

The other puppy is shrieking in the exercise room, Laurie's hand is pouring blood, and I'm panting like a basset hound that just treed a raccoon.

I manage to gasp: "What in hell is going on?"

"THE PUPPY," Laurie screams. "THE PUPPY IS CAUGHT ON THE TREADMILL.

YOU'VE GOT TO HELP HER. HURRY!"

This is not what I had pictured.

"What?" One of my typically intelligent replies in situations like this.

"THE PUPPY. THE PUPPY IS CAUGHT ON THE TREADMILL. I COULDN'T MAKE IT STOP. HELP HER…..HURRY…SHE'S HURT!!!!"

Laurie had been walking on the treadmill when one of our puppies had jumped on the machine.

Somehow, the puppy's leg had gotten caught under the track.

The poor thing was trapped, squealing, trying to break free.

When Laurie finally got the treadmill stopped, she was faced with trying to get the dog's leg out, with no success.

Hence, the screaming.

The puppy, in panic and pain, had been biting Laurie's hand constantly as she tried to free the leg.

There was a lot of blood.

As I assess the situation, I'm sure we now have a three-legged dog, but I don't want to make the situation any worse.

I'm bending over the treadmill, trying to free Rose's leg, when I look up to see our neighbor, Dorrie, coming across the yard.

She had heard the screaming and was coming to help.

I might mention here that she had been holding a ladder for her husband, Barney, who was working on a carving he had placed in a tree when the screaming started.

Barney was left in the tree.

Dorrie, God love 'er, was on her way to help.

I never followed up to see how long Barney stayed in that tree, but I've seen him since the incident, so I guess he got down all right.

Anyway, as Dorrie heads across the lawn, I tell Laurie to shut the sauna door.

"I'm naked…ya know."

"DON'T WORRY ABOUT THAT. JUST GET ROSE OUT OF THERE. OMIGOD, I KNOW SHE'S LOST HER LEG. IS HER LEG STILL THERE?"

"Laurie…" I try to get through to her in a calm tone. "Dorrie will be screaming louder than the dog if she walks in on this. Shut the door."

After glancing at the scene in front of her……fat guy, naked, gun, blood, screaming……Laurie finally comes to her senses enough to realize that maybe she should meet Dorrie on the deck.

In the meantime, poor Rose is trying to chew off my hand at the wrist while I wrestle with her leg, which is solidly jammed between the track and the roller.

I'm sure this poor little thing has lost her leg when……BOOM….her leg pops free.

Rose is out the door like a shot, yipping at the top of her lungs as she rips past Laurie and Dorrie, then dives underneath the deck.

I come tearing around the corner yelling: "DON'T LOOK DORRIE!!!!"

It was too late.

She'd already been stunned.

So….. here's the new picture.

Now we have a fat guy with a towel wrapped around him, as best we could, on hands and knees, digging under the deck, trying to convince an injured, hysterical, puppy that it would be a good idea to come out so we can take care of her.

She had that "no thanks" look about her.

I looked up on the deck to see her brother, Rocky, peeking around the door.

He seemed to be asking: "How's it goin' out there?"

Rock headed for the water dish while the three of us, me, Dorrie and Laurie, kept trying to convince Rose to come out from under the deck.

We're all terrified that when she does come out, she will have only three legs.

I imagine the neighbors were wondering what in the world was happening at the Perkins.

"Looks like he's out there wrapped in a yellow towel….diggin' in the dirt."

Well, I guess that was true, to a point.

Finally, Laurie coaxed out "The Rose" with a bacon rind.

She picked her up and came to me, sniffling.

"Look at her leg….I can't.

Is it still there?"

I couldn't bring myself to look either, but since Rose was now calmly chewing on the bacon rind, I thought there was hope.

OH MAN!

The leg was there.

The blood came from Laurie's hand.

An emergency call to the vet and we're off on a high speed run to fix the leg of "The Rose."

She was a good girl.

Amazingly, the break was minor.

The vet tells us it will heal in a short time.

Now our attention turns to Laurie.

Her hand is looking real bad.

ZOOM.

We're off to another Emergency Room.

Now, on any other Sunday afternoon, the Emergency Room is no doubt very quiet.

We arrive with a seriously lacerated hand to find at least 30 people waiting for treatment.

"Never mind this," I tell Laurie. "I'll wait in the car with the dogs and read the paper until they take care of you."

I turn on the air conditioning to ice down the dogs….the car starts to overheat.

It's 90 degrees.

Shut down the car……the dogs start to overheat.

Air conditioning back on…..car overheats.

WHAT A CIRCUS!

By the way, I've upgraded my wardrobe at this point to a bathrobe and slippers.

I can't take off the bathrobe because.....well....you know the earlier situation.

So.....the windows are all down....I'm reading the paper, and the vision in my left eye gets fuzzy.

I blink several times, but it doesn't get any better.

What would one think in a situation like this?

"OMIGOD...IT'S A STROKE."

My turn to panic.

I throw open the car door and head for the Emergency Room....robe and slippers flapping.

I'm thinking I have just minutes left as I put my hand in the pocket of my robe and find......the lens from my glasses.

"What the............?"

While I was reading the paper, the left eye lens had fallen out of my glasses and into the pocket of my robe.

No stroke.....just a loose screw.

I'm in a pool of stress induced sweat as Laurie comes out of the Emergency Room.

"Everything go ok?" she asks. "You'll have to drive, I can't do it with this hand."

At this point, I could only stare.

It's an hour back home.

We cover the distance with my left eye closed, squinting into the sun with my good eye, with Laurie and the dogs looking on with undisguised amusement.

My robe kept falling open, so I had to keep that closed.

In my mind, what was left of it, I was trying to come up with a workable explanation in the event a police officer had stopped us on the trip home.

There was none.

It was brutal.

We pulled into the driveway near dark.

The two puppies, as only little bundles of fur can do as they reach for your heart, give me an adoring look that says: "Ya got any more of those bacon rinds?"

I reached into the pocket of my robe.

The three of us are sitting in the car, calmly chewing on a bacon rind, when Laurie walks by, pats each of the puppies on the head, then pats me on the head and says: "Happy Father's Day."

Show Dogs

SHOW DOGS

In my continuing quest to find the perfect television program, I again spent an entire evening speed surfing through the channels, until the Westminster Dog Show caught my eye.

WOW!!

What a classy, first class, dog show.

There's a passel of beautiful dogs romping through the show, including a stunning pair of Lhasa Apsos.

These little darlings came prancing before the judges in perfect rhythm, with ribbons holding tufts of hair in a perfect top knot, and the rest of their body perfectly manicured.

Their long side hair, beautifully trimmed, brushed the floor as they gave the judges their best shot.

Their toenails, clipped to perfection, made a clicking sound as they made the turn after passing the judges stand.

At that point, the handler turned the dogs toward the judges, allowing them both to sit, in unison, and await the result.

Incredible!

Perfect dogs!

Perfect discipline!

Well, we have a pair of Lhasa Apsos, so I'm thinking we should consider entering the hounds in the Westminster Dog Show.

As I'm thinking this, I hear a wailing and a gnashing of teeth.

Rocky and Rose come flying into the den like one ball of fur, rolling over each other as they try to get the best shot at giving the other a good nip.

They roll all the way across the room, snarling and barking, hit the couch, bounce off, then take a moment to stare at each other, panting, with tongue hanging out, and drool dripping on the floor.

Rose has one ear flipped on top of her head and Rocky is missing a tuft of hair from his tail.

Moments later they're a blur of motion again, snarling and barking, fighting their way back out of the den, across the dining room, through the kitchen, and up the stairs.

Just out of curiosity, I trudge up the stairs to see if there are any serious injuries.

Rock and Rose are sitting on the bed, licking each others whiskers.

At this point, I'm not sure if they're cut out to be show dogs.

Rose looks up with the "Dad's here" look, which causes both of them to jump off the bed and begin pulling and nipping at my trousers.

I can already see that the discipline part is going to be a problem for these show dogs.

They can be a bit intense from time to time.

Last summer, we stopped at this quaint little roadside stand to buy some fresh strawberries and sweet corn.

As I prepare to leave the car, I notice a yellow Lab quietly walk out from behind the stand and circle in front of our vehicle.

Rock was on it immediately and started to tremble and whine.

Rose gave him the look.

"You on one? Where's it at? I don't see it."

I'm dumb enough to still be thinking this is not big deal.

WRONG....biscuit breath.

Laurie and I are thinking the Lab has trotted off into the field when Cujo suddenly slams against the window on Laurie's side, fangs exposed, lips back, snarling and scratching, foam dropping from his mouth as he tries to get at Rock and Rose.

I soiled myself.

Laurie, who was terrified, was trying to hold back our dynamic duo, who also were frightened by the attack, but still trying to get at the Lab through the closed window.

I grabbed Rocky to get him out of the action, but he gave me a snarl that said: "I'm kickin' somebody's ass. It's going to be you or that crazy dog!"

I tossed him back at Laurie.

Now she's caught in the crossfire, trying to hold back our dogs while Cujo is slobbering at the window next to her ear, trying to get a piece of all four of us.

I'm sure he's thinking: "Roll down that window and I'll show ya who's yer daddy."

At this point the farmer comes at a dead run, grabs the collar of the Lab, and pulls him out of the fight, snarling and coughing.

Rock and Rose are still bouncing off the window, trying to get at the Lab.

The farmer says: "He won't hurtcha. He's just playin'."

I give the farmer an incredulous look as I try to hold Rose, who is now kicking and scratching me in a very vital area.

Cujo sniffs twice and gives our hounds a look that says: "Come on back, bring your buddies, without the chick and the fat guy."

The lab strolls off toward the corn field, glancing back over his shoulder with a sneer.

The farmer wants me to look at his strawberries, I'm looking for an outhouse.

His strawberries were that last things I wanted to see.

By now Rose has lost interest in the fight and Rock is in the back seat, licking his butt.

Now that is NOT going to score points at the Westminster Dog Show.

Incidentally, I've been working with Rock on that butt-lickin' deal for the past several months.

My mantra has been….. "Lick my face FIRST….THEN the butt."

He still isn't getting passing grades in that class.

By the way, we did not buy any corn or strawberries from Cujo and his handler.

So I'm thinking about these various instances as we sit down in our den to consider filling out an application for the Westminster Dog Show.

Rose walks into the room and starts gnawing on my slipper, followed by Rock, who has somehow gotten into a jar of maple syrup. There's syrup dripping from his beard and he's making perfect maple syrup paw prints as he strolls across our carpet.

He jumps in my lap and rubs his beard on my shirt.

This is not show dog behavior, but ya gotta love the Rock.

All in all, after debating the strengths and weaknesses of our dogs, we have decided they're not cut out to be show dogs.

Our hounds, I'm afraid, don't have the refinement necessary for the big show.

They'd probably wind up getting the thumb.

I can picture the two of them prancing into the hall, chests out, looking over the competition.

Unfortunately, I can also picture Rose looking sideways at Rock as they cruise by the judges and saying: "Look at the top knot on that snooty bitch by the poodle. I'll bet it's a wig."

Potty mouth….DQ'ed!

ROCKY'S DREAM

I had a dream last night.

My boy Rocky, who is constantly tugging and pulling at his leash when we take him for a walk, had slipped his collar over his head.

The Rock took off at a dead run across a meadow, then stood at the edge of a forest, peering into the trees.

I could feel the fear in the pit of my stomach.

"Rock…don't go in the woods!" I yelled across the meadow. "You don't know what's in there!"

The Rock looked at me, then at the woods, back at me again, and then leaped into the trees, disappearing from sight in seconds.

I was holding our other dog, Rose. We started off across the meadow at a dead run.

"No!" I yelled. "He's not ready for this. He's too small!"

I could hear Rocky barking when Rose and I got to the edge of the woods, but I couldn't see him.

I yelled to him: "Come on Rock, follow my voice, get out of there."

Rose was barking hysterically in my arms.

Both of us felt a fear that we really didn't understand.

Then the sound of Rocky's bark changed from a "good to be free" bark to a frightened pitch.

I suppose all of us who have pets get to know their personalities and voice inflections, just like our children.

In the meadow I looked down and a kennel, with strong metal bars, had magically appeared.

I took Rose, placed her in the kennel and said: "You'll be safe here Rosie. I have to find Rocky."

There was a massive padlock on the kennel with a huge key.

I locked the kennel, placed the key in my pocket, and looked at the woods.

That unexplainable fear was still nagging in the pit of my stomach.

I plunged into the deep woods, pushing back brush and branches while yelling at the top of my voice: "I'll find you Rock. No matter where you are, I'll find you!"

His barking seemed to be getting further away.

"Why didn't I check that collar better?" I questioned myself as I stumbled through the woods, trying to follow the sound of Rocky's bark.

"This is my fault, I should have checked his collar better."

The tears were back again as I flogged myself for allowing this to happen.

Rocky's bark was less frequent now and growing very faint.

I picked up the pace and started running through the thick underbrush, terrified that I would lose the sound of his bark, terrified that he was alone and frightened.

Suddenly, I burst into another open meadow.

Rocky was sitting on the other side of the meadow.

There was a bald eagle in a tree just above him.

On the left, a wolf was approaching Rock, while another wolf was approaching from the right.

Rocky wasn't making a sound, but I could see his body was quivering with fear.

The haunches were up on the wolves, their tongues hanging out, and drool was rolling off their chops as they steadily advanced toward Rock.

My fear immediately turned to anger.

"Not today," I yelled at the wolves. "You won't hurt him today!"

The eagle spread its wings and flew off the tree branch, swooping and diving at the wolves as it flew cover over Rocky.

The wolves stopped in their tracks.

"Stay there Rock, I'm coming for you!"

There was no more fear as I walked across the meadow, never taking my eyes from the wolves.

The eagle made one final swoop over the wolves, then circled over my head one time before landing on my right shoulder.

Strangely enough, the talons of this magnificent bird caused no pain as they dug into my shoulder. I could feel nothing of its massive weight as we walked across the meadow.

The closer we got to Rocky, the further the wolves backed off.

As we got to his side, I looked at the wolves and said: "One or both of you, come on, but you won't harm anyone today."

The wolves backed off until they disappeared in the woods.

I reached down to pick up Rocky.

He was crying when he looked up at me.

"I was really afraid." he said.

"I know buddy, I was too, but we're ok now. Let's go home."

He jumped into my arms and nuzzled into my neck as we headed back to pick up Rose.

The eagle launched off my shoulder and circled over our heads as we made our way out of the deep woods.

When we came out of the woods, the metal cage was gone, so was the eagle.

Laurie was sitting in the meadow, stretched out in a lawn chair, reading a book, with Rose quietly napping in her lap.

She looked up and said: "Where have you guys been?"

Rose didn't even look up.

Rocky and I looked at each other and said: "We just went for a walk."

Now, you'd think Laurie would have been a little surprised that Rocky was talking to her, but she wasn't.

I don't understand how she got Rose out of that kennel either.

Go figure.

I don't normally remember dreams, but this one was very vivid the next morning.

My first thought was that I'm getting way too close to these dogs, but I rationalized to myself that there must be some meaning in this dream.

So….the next morning I'm sitting in the den, having a cup of coffee, trying to sort out the lofty and poignant meaning buried deep within last nights dream.

Rock leaps up on my lap, licks my face, and nuzzles into my neck.

I confess that I'm glad Rock didn't talk out loud, although a talking dog would be the talk of the town, but I could feel him saying: "Thanks for saving me from the bad guys and getting me out of the woods. I love ya."

He curled up on my lap and went to sleep.

Turns out the dream wasn't all that complicated.

We just need to know there is someone in our lives who is willing to keep us safe and find us when we're lost.

It's one less thing to worry about.

Thanks Rock.

COORS....HERE'S TO YA!

My buddy, Coors, died today.

I feel the loss and my heart hurts, but he had a good run....he was 91 in human years.

In all honesty, I must confess that I wasn't totally shocked.

His age was catching up to him.

Those of us who loved him knew that, but we didn't want to see him go.

Just a few days ago, he came up and put his head in my lap.

I could see he was tired.

A few days later, his heart just couldn't keep up anymore.

It was his time.

He needed someone to make a decision for him. Coors was fortunate that someone loved him enough to make that decision, but that doesn't make the pain any less.

Coors was a beautiful Golden Retriever.

His coat and muzzle had aged and become a distinguished grey over the years, but Coors still was a stately gentleman....a patriarch in the home of Jim and Ceil Held.

From the time he was a fuzzy little puppy, he wanted to be involved in everything.

This past fall, Coors was working in a supervisory position as Jim and I put together the materials for a deer hunting blind to be built deep in the woods....a goodly distance from the house.

As we prepared to move the material, Coors came up to me and nuzzled my hand, making it clear he wanted to go along.

His bones were too old and stiff to run with us, so I made room in the gator for Coors to jump up and sit beside me.

As he wiggled those old bones getting comfortable, his eyes were locked on Jim.

Guess he wanted to make sure he took the right trail.

When we got the construction project underway, Jim needed to go back to the house to get some additional tools, which left Coors and me enjoying a beautiful fall afternoon.

Coors was still sitting beside me in the gator, sniffing the air and seeming to enjoy being out in the woods.

Just up the trail, a doe popped out of the woods and stared at us.

Coors snuffed a bit, then gingerly stepped out of the gator and limped a few yards toward the doe.

He looked back at me, then turned around and got back in the gator beside me.

Coors was telling me: "Not today, maybe a few years ago, but not today."

I stroked his head and said: "I know. I feel that way some days too."

Coors put his head in my lap and fell asleep until Jim returned.

I held my buddy tight during that brief nap.

Coors was a dear friend to Jim and Ceil for some 14 years.

He held court every night from his personal recliner, he rode shotgun with Jim along the back roads, and he spent afternoons watching his favorite soap opera.

Coors was everyone's friend.

I shall miss those days sitting at the counter in Coors' house, with him sitting beside me, nuzzling my hand until I took the time to scratch behind his ears.

Coors was a good lad….a good friend.

He loved everyone….and we all loved Coors.

So…..although our hearts hurt because he is no longer here, we celebrate the life of Coors and we're grateful for the love he showed, without qualification, without question.

He had a good and a long life.

More importantly, Coors made a difference in the Held family.

In the final analysis, I guess that's all any of us can hope for when our clock winds down.

Like Coors, I hope we all have a chance to make a difference.

Like Coors, I hope we all have someone to love us without qualification.

Like Coors, I hope we all live to be old dogs.

SUP DOG

I must confess that, while I love her without reservation, I still have a communication gap with at least one of my daughters.

Even though she is now into her 30's, a good share of the time I have no idea what the hell she's talking about when we visit.

Last night, I picked up the phone and was greeted by: "Sup?"

"What?"

"Sup?"

"Is this a crank call?"

"Dad, you and mom...seriously...have really got to get with it. What's up?"

"My blood pressure, that's what's up! Why don't you speak in easy to understand phrases?"

"Whatever. It's all good."

"What's all good?"

"It's all good."

"WHAT'S ALL GOOD!"

"It's ALL good."

"WHAT?"

I felt like I was in an Abbot and Costello routine.

I fully expected the next response to be: "He's on third."

Instead, the answer I got was: "Dude, it's a phrase. It means things are going well in my world."

"Then why don't you say that?"

"I don't know. Anyway………………….."

Long silence, no response.

"Anyway what?"

"Anyway, it's all good."

There's no hope.

This is a very intelligent woman. She is a professional who holds two difficult to obtain degrees.

I just don't get it.

Maybe it's me.

I could tell she was distracted, so I asked her what was absorbing her attention.

"I'm texting. Gotta keep in contact with everyone."

"Why don't you concentrate on one communication form at a time when you visit with your mother and me?"

"Whatever."

Things were going downhill, so I gave up on our conversation.

"I'm going to give the phone to your mother."

"Awesome. Love ya."

Honest to God, it's like she operates in a parallel universe.

I think Laurie must speak the language, because the two of them carried on a conversation for more than a half hour before the call ended.

"Mom, gotta go. Gotta check MySpace to see what everyone did over the weekend. Love ya."

Now…this MySpace is a new deal to me.

Apparently, it's a place on the internet where the younger crowd spend time visiting on-line.

I would have checked it out, but my computer skills have never advanced beyond the "on" button.

However, my mind did wander to what my entry would read if I was talking about my weekend on MySpace:

Went to the dump on Saturday. Had a chance to visit with Bobby.
He is so totally awesome…ya know what I mean?
I was really amped after dumping the recyclables.
Stopped for breakfast with the boys on the way home.
Gnarly bunch…that breakfast club. Love 'em.
We had a great time talkin' about taxes,
settled all the political issues, and a lotta other stuff.
I was really stoked on the way home.
Got home and found out Laurie had a bunch of errands she wanted done.
What a buzz killer!
Got two poops and two pees when I walked the dogs.

BOOYAH!

We were rockin' the patch!!

Tough to get over the adrenaline rush when ya got something like that workin' for ya, so I went to bed at nine.

I was like…totally tired after such a tough day.

Gotta run.

Somehow, I don't think people would be waiting in line to read about my weekend, but that's how I roll.

Anyway……after going to bed at nine, I wake up at three o'clock the next morning and limp down the stairs to grab a glass of milk.

You can imagine my surprise when I find Laurie already downstairs, sitting at the counter.

"Sup?" she says.

OH………MY………GOD!

She's been infected!

"Whatcha doin' up, Dude?"

Now I'm intimidated.

With my head hanging down, I respond: "Just coming down for a glass of milk."

"Yeah…me too. Try the chocolate. It's gnarly."

Quietly, head down, staring at the floor, I ask: "What have you done with my wife?"

"Lighten up Dude. It's all good."

Still staring at the floor, I ask again: "No, really, where is Laurie?"

"Right here Sparky, just trippin' on milk and peanut butter."

"Listen, I know Laurie, I live with Laurie, YOU are not Laurie."

She licked a gob of peanut butter off the end of a butter knife and said: "Whatever."

Now the back door opens and Bobby comes in with two plastic garbage cans.

"Hey Homer…Sup? Ya forgot the cans."

"Bobby, it's three in the morning!"

"No problem Red Ryder. Woulda been here earlier, but I got tied up texting my posse."

"Your posse?"

"Yea….my boys. We're kickin' it all the time. That's the way we roll."

I'm standing in the kitchen with my mouth open, thinking these two are a few clowns short of a circus, when one of the boys from the breakfast club rolls in.

It's DJ.

He has his cap on backward and he's wearing those pants that damn near fall off your butt.

"Sup Dog?" he asks.

This must be something new.

What kind of an animal is a "Sup Dog?"

The question apparently calls for some sort of response.

Laurie, who is now elbow deep in a tub of ice cream, says: "Ain't nothin' Dog. Just livin' the dream. It's all good."

The room started spinning.

The last conscious thought I had before I blacked out was wondering how I was going to get my wife back.

The next thing I remember is Laurie shaking me and saying: "What's wrong? You were mumbling something about a dog. Are you OK?"

I looked around and found myself safely tucked into bed, Rock and Rose were curled up beside me, and most importantly, Laurie was next to me in her flannel pajamas and she's speaking my language.

Oh baby……what a relief!

It was just a dream!!!

Now that it's over I guess it's all good, but I don't want to go through another night like that….ya know what I'm sayin'?

Dude, it was like…..too intense…..SERIOUSLY!
Whatever.
Anyway…………
Gotta go.
Love ya!

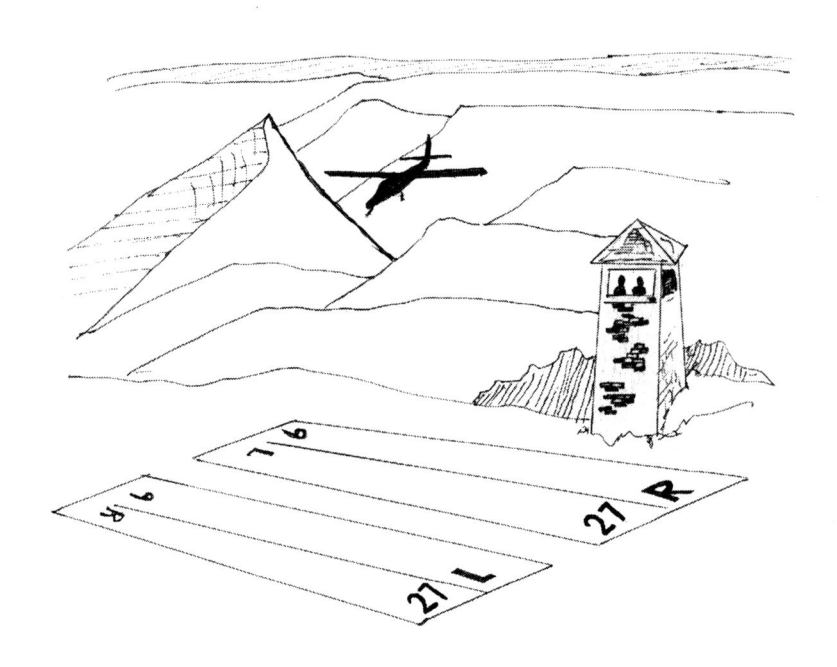

The Right Direction

THE RIGHT DIRECTION

I suppose all of us lose our sense of direction at some point in our life.

I have.

How important it is at those times to have someone to guide us back on the right path, to help us make the right decisions.

The point is always driven home for me when I recall the training I received to fly an airplane.

Early on in the training, it seemed a waste of time to be going through those endless hours learning about weight and balance, how an airplane engine operates, proper ways to communicate, and how to remain calm in an emergency.

Over and over again, the same situations.

I wanted to fly, so let's get in the aircraft.

Little did I know how critically important it is to first have the ability to handle all the little details, seemingly minor details, like doing a pre-flight inspection the same way every time, before moving on to bigger things.

Ignoring the little details all too frequently will spawn big time problems.

The constant repetition of my training, both on the ground and in the air, taught me to react to certain situations without thinking about it, while remaining calm.

It all came together when I had the opportunity to take my first solo cross country flight.

The adrenaline was pumping through my body when I started the aircraft after going through the pre-flight check.

I keyed the microphone and called the controller: "Cessna Four Four Two Yankee Whiskey, ready for taxi to the active."

Another rush when the controller responded: "Four Two Yankee Whiskey…cleared for taxi."

My mind is racing with all of the information the instructors have jammed into my head up to this point.

Am I missing anything?

Are my charts correct?

Are my timing plots exacting enough to bring me to that little speck of an airport more than 100 miles away?

The Cessna slowly nosed up to the number one position for departure.

I keyed the mike again.

"Cessna Four Four Two Yankee Whiskey, holding short on two eight with Bravo. We'll be departing to the South."

"Yankee Whiskey, cleared for take-off on two eight....South Departure."

Trying to keep my voice calm and professional, I responded: "Four Two Yankee Whiskey, rolling on two eight…South departure."

Releasing the toe brakes, I opened the throttles and started rolling down the center line of the runway.

Talking to myself, I counted off…….40….45…50…..55 knots….. rotate!

Pulling back on the yoke, I felt the wheels lift off as I began my climb at 80 knots.

Unless you have been at the controls of an aircraft, you can't explain the exhilaration you feel at lift off.

You are in control of a flying machine and you're responsible for getting it back on the ground.

This is the ultimate in taking responsibility for yourself.

As we roll off to the South, the work of a pilot begins as I check my instruments…. speed, heading, and altitude…then set my timer enroute to a small airport more than 100 miles away.

The confidence builds as I hit my first check point right on time and on the money.

Ten minutes later, the confidence ratchets up another notch when I hit the second checkpoint, on time and on the spot.

Now overconfidence is a factor.

I allowed myself to become a tourist, and lost my focus.

Not a good idea…in life or in an airplane.

The next checkpoint is on time, but the target is off to the East.

No problem, correct the wind drift and we'll be back on target at the next checkpoint.

I gazed at the desert floor passing below me and watched several Condors riding the wind currents.

The next check point was a few minutes off projected arrival time. The target was barely visible to the East.

It was painfully obvious that I had become over confident and not done a good job in correcting the wind drift, but rather than admit my mistake and ask for help, I decided that I would ride it out, since the airport was less then twenty minutes ahead and off to the East.

It becomes dangerous very quickly if we minimize a situation and don't ask for help in correcting the problem.

When I reached the target mark for the airport, there's nothing in sight.

Rationalizing that my timing was off, I continued to the South for another 15 minutes.

Still no airport, and I'm now heading for Mexico.

Realizing I'm lost, it's time to swallow my pride and ask for help, but thanks to my training, there's no panic.

I knew I had adequate fuel and I knew the emergency procedures.

Adjusting my telemetry to ride a radio signal to a major airport I knew would be to the East, I watched the needle adjust and followed the trail.

When I knew I was close enough for a radio transmission, I asked for help.

The calm voice of a ground controller came back: "Turn to and maintain a heading of two-seven-zero. The airport will be at your two o'clock in ten."

In ten (minutes), the airport was at my two o'clock.

The local controller came on the radio: "Four Two Yankee Whiskey, good to have you with us, cleared to land on nine right."

As I shut down the aircraft, I was patting myself on the back for remaining calm during the emergency when I noticed my shirt was totally drenched.

That old adage, "Never let 'em see you sweat," didn't apply.

We all learn lessons every day.

In that one flight I learned why it is necessary to do things over and over again until you get it right.

I learned why the instructor would give me an in-flight emergency during a training flight and expect me to solve it.

I learned that I have to take responsibility for every decision I make, right or wrong.

I learned to ask for help.

Thankfully, there was a calm voice on the other end when I needed it, telling me to "turn to and maintain a heading of two-seven-zero".......the right direction.

We all face situations every day when we need help, when we need direction, but all too frequently we allow our pride to overcome our common sense and try to "ride it out."

Sometimes we can't "ride it out."

Sometimes we need only a small correction to turn us back to the right heading…to the right direction.

Sometimes we need to ask for help.

In those times, don't let your pride overcome common sense.

Ask for help!

Someone will be there to answer.

"Turn to and maintain a heading of two-seven-zero….the airport will be at your two o'clock in ten."

Put your flaps down and turn your nose to the wind….you'll touch down on Nine Right.

Welcome home!

TANGO LIMA

I went to a Celebration of Life recently for a man I had never met.

By the time I left, I felt I had known him all his life, thanks to the many stories shared by his family, friends, and co-workers.

From the young man who was taught how to properly clean an aircraft windscreen when he was a new employee to the former military pilot who trusted him to fly five feet off his wing in photo shoots, it was obvious this was a man who made a difference in his lifetime.

He had time for everyone.

From the friend who watched him make "angels" in the snow during a recent snowstorm to the glowing letters his parents and Company received from locations across the globe, it was obvious this was a man who cared about others.

This was a person who loved his life and the people in it....all of them.

This was a person who created memories.

The stories went on and on, all of them inspirational.

From his love of deep water fishing and bird hunting, to his mastery of cooking and love of sushi.... he didn't miss a moment.

This was a person who attacked life and shook out all the loose change.

Whatever was out there for him, he embraced it, with a vengeance.

Everyone loved this man, including his uncle, who learned of his independent nature early in life.

As I recall the story, there was an attempt to get him to stop sucking his thumb, but he came up to his uncle, thumb in mouth, and said: "I think what I do on my own time is my business."

He was five years old at the time.

This man was an individual, an innovator, a leader, and quite obviously from the stories we heard, a wonderful person to count as your friend.

It is inspiring to attend such an event and listen to positive stories of a life well-lived.

This was a special person.

It was an uplifting afternoon.

As I left the airport hangar where the Celebration of Life was held, I had this mental picture of a man flying an aircraft through heavy fog.

Visibility is zero-zero.

The instrument panel is lit, but there is no global positioning system, no airspeed indicator, no artificial horizon, no altitude indicator, no throttle.... just a compass and a radio.

A voice comes over the radio: "Tango Lima...this is Kingdom One approach control.

Please squawk your position."

"Tango Lima. Unsure of our position."

"Tango Lima...We are with you. Turn to and maintain three-six-zero. We've had you on our radar for 41 years. Your life has come full circle. We'll call your final."

"Tango Lima....turning to three-six-zero."

When the fog bound aircraft reaches the mark at three-six-zero, the fog clears, allowing the aircraft to enter a beautiful, sun filled, afternoon, with bright green fields below, intersected by winding rivers that look like a ribbon of blue trailing through the countryside.

Above the aircraft is a cloudless blue sky.

"Tango Lima....Kingdom One air traffic control. Do you have the field in sight?"

"Tango Lima....field in sight. It's beautiful!"

"Tango Lima...maintain three-six-zero. You're cleared to land straight-in on three-six. Airspeed is not a factor."

"Tango Lima. Straight-in on three-six. Airspeed no factor."

The aircraft floats over the numbers and makes an unassisted, pillow soft, landing, then turns off the main runway onto a taxiway and holds short, awaiting instruction.

"Tango Lima....Kingdom One ground control. Welcome home. A guide truck is enroute."

The pilot acknowledges: "Tango Lima."

As the guide truck pulls up, the pilot looks down to see the throttle has re-appeared in the aircraft.

A radio transmission comes from the guide truck.

"Tango Lima....you have the aircraft. Throttle up. I'll show you the way."

"Tango Lima. Throttling up."

As the aircraft slides in smoothly behind the guide truck with "Tango Lima" at the controls, we look through the windscreen and see the pilot.

"Tango Lima" has that infectious smile, beaming wide, as he throttles up.

He's beginning a new adventure…..and he's ready for what lies ahead.

My final thought is on that guide truck.

I recognize the driver.

I have seen him and his truck many times in my life, particularly when I have faced tough times and difficult bumps in the road.

He always seems to be there at those times….showing me the way.

I also recognize the sign on that truck.

I have seen it many times in my life.

It says: FOLLOW ME.

FLYING IN FORMATION

I was sitting on our deck yesterday, staring off into the distance, when a flock of Canadian geese made a low level pass, at treetop height, in their perfect "V" formation.

It seemed they were floating, their wings locked into position, as they moved off to the northwest.

The beauty of it all makes me shiver.

I watch these magnificent creatures in the Spring and Fall, and I have wondered why they always fly in that perfect formation.

As most things in life, the answer isn't all that complex.

As each goose flaps its wings, it creates lift for the trailing bird, making it possible for the flock to fly further before it tires.

When the flock flies in that perfect "V" formation, it increases its range by 71-percent, as opposed to each goose going it alone.

WORKING TOGETHER TO ACCOMPLISH MORE.

What a unique concept.

I guess we could all take a lesson from that.

When the lead goose gets tired, it rotates to the back of the formation, while the next in line steps up to take the lead.

The lead goose knows when it's had enough, when staying up front would become a detriment to the flock, and it steps aside for the stronger and more rested member of the group.

The next in line doesn't hesitate to move forward.

The flock doesn't miss a beat.

SHARED LEADERSHIP AND RESPONSIBILITY.

I guess we could all take a lesson from that.

I even learned, during a brief bit of research, that Canadian geese are cheerleaders.

Those in the rear honk to encourage those at the point to keep up their speed.

POSITIVE RE-INFORCEMENT.

I guess we could all take a lesson from that.

Ya know, when you think about it, I guess it is important that the geese honking from behind are building positive re-enforcement.

Otherwise, it's just another annoying honk, and we all hear enough of those every day.

IF YOU CAN'T SAY ANYTHING POSITIVE…SHUT UP.

I guess we could all take a lesson from that.

Here's another interesting fact about Canadian geese.

When one is sick or wounded, two other geese will drop out of formation and follow the sick or wounded bird to the ground in order to provide protection.

They will stay with the injured bird until it gets well or dies...and only then will the protectors hook up with another flock or try to catch up to their own.

ABSOLUTE....UNQUESTIONED....LOYALTY.

I guess we could all take a lesson from that.

I wonder, in this ego-driven, "me-first," world of instant gratification, how many of us would be willing to fly in formation, share the leadership and recognition, applaud our peers for their efforts, and maintain absolute loyalty to the flock.

How many of us would fall out of formation to circle over a wounded friend, then sit beside that friend 24 hours a day until the crisis resolves itself?

Matter of fact, what would you do if you knew you were next in line to drop out of formation, leaving the flock move on, while you attend to a sick or wounded companion?

Would you try to duck the responsibility and look for someone to take your place?

What if you were the sick or wounded goose?

Would you trust your companions to fly cover for you and attend to your needs?

COMPLETE TRUST.

I guess we could all take a lesson from that.

That injured or sick goose never has to worry about companions being there when they are needed.

The geese flying protection don't delegate responsibility, they take responsibility...for themselves...for their actions....for their companion.

They do it without question.

They do it because it is their turn....they do it because it is expected of them.

PERSONAL RESPONSIBILITY...MEETING EXPECTATIONS.

I guess we could all take a lesson from that.

They are, the Canadian geese, magnificent creatures.

All too often, I fear, we are not.

My dad had a pet phrase when he got angry: "You've got the brains of a goose!"

I never took that as a compliment….until now.

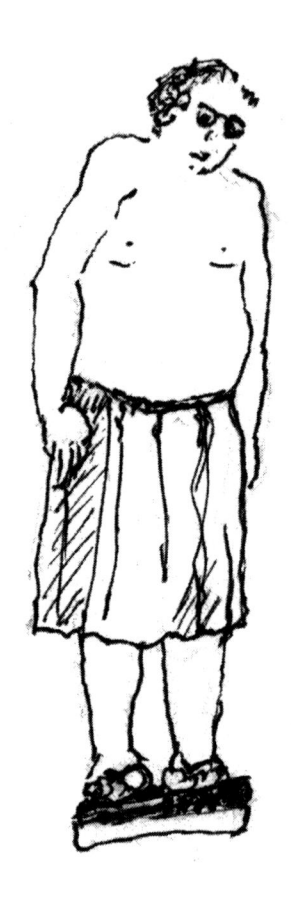

Porker

PORKER

I can't understand it!

I hardly eat a thing, but I still gain weight.

Lately, when I do get on one of those miserable scales, it says: "One at a time!"

No more talking scales.

This morning I got on the beast and it said 298….that's right….298…. two pounds short of 300.

"What the……….?" My voice trails off as the shock sets in.

I picked up the scale and looked at the bottom.

"Gotta be defective!!"

I shook it like a rag doll.

"I hardly eat a thing!" I thought to myself as I grabbed a tootsie roll and headed down the stairs.

I hammered down the tootsie roll as I pondered this problem.

It was quite obvious that we needed a new scale.

Told my wife: "There's something wrong with the scale." I said. "Looks like its reading about 80 pounds heavy."

She just stared at me….mouth open.

Laurie was baking cookies, so I grabbed a few, six, and waddled back upstairs to take a shower.

Cookie crumbs were tangled in my chest hair as the water heater worked overtime to hose off this 300-pound hog of a body.

"Maybe I have bad metabolism," I whined to myself.

"Don't understand it…I eat like a bird."

When I stepped out of the shower and bent over to grab a towel, water started running out of my bellybutton.

NOW THIS WAS TOO MUCH!

After I caught my breath from bending over, the drying process began.

It took three towels and a hair dryer.

"Ya know," I said to Laurie, "I'm big boned, that probably accounts for a lot of this weight."

I got an incredulous look and a one word answer: "Right!"

I glared at her as I grabbed a frozen Snickers bar from the freezer.

"I hardly eat a thing. I think someone has been force feeding me doughnuts when I sleep."

Again, the look and the response: "Right!"

I gave her another glare, wiped chocolate from my chin and asked: "When's lunch?"

BOOM!!!

Two hamburgers and fried potatoes magically appear.

Thinking thin, I said: "Ya know, I don't need two hamburgers if I'm going to lose weight." I said that to myself.

I pounded down the first hamburger and fried potatoes, gave the second hamburger an eyeball, then grabbed it and headed out the door.

"It's small, how bad can it hurt me?"

After a brutal walk to the Post Office, I return to find chocolate pudding, with whipped cream, on the counter.

Not wanting to be rude, I slammed it down.

"I just can't understand this weight deal, considering how little I eat in a day."

While I'm thinking about this, I pound down three rice krispie bars.

"It's gotta be metabolism."

I suppose I could try a diet, but there's nothing magic about diets.

I'm great at starting diets, usually every morning, but I'm hungry by noon and ... POOF ... the diet disappears for another day.

Anyway, I trudge back upstairs, nibbling on a piece of string cheese, and grab a pair of loafers I haven't worn in a while.

"What the…………...?" My voice trails off again.

The leather has shrunk!

It took awhile to get my fat feet jammed into the cowhide.

Immediately looking for someone to blame, I yell down the stairs: "Laurie, what did you do to these shoes?"

She gives me the stink eye, without the courtesy of a response.

As I left the house for a meeting I grabbed several cookies, eight, "for the road."

Laurie was mumbling something about the "Lardashe" logo on my slacks as I slipped out the door, trailing cookie crumbs.

Funny, I don't recall that label.

By now, my eyes are tearing up from the pain in my feet, but I figured my slacks, which, incidentally, had shrunk, would cut off the circulation to my legs as soon as I sat down in the car, which would do away with the pain in my feet.

Life is a series of trade-offs.

There was a box of milk duds on the passenger seat, so I snacked on a few as I backed out of the driveway.

This weight thing is just a mystery to me.

The committee meeting was one of those endless affairs, with participants who dart off on a tangent every few minutes that has nothing to do with the agenda.

We're sitting on these flimsy, plastic, chairs.

Mine was snug.

I decided to leave early, so I stood up.

"What the................?" My voice trailed off as I looked behind me.

The chair was stuck to my ass.

It's hard to make a dignified exit when you have to peel the chair off your ass before leaving.

Anyway, I'm chuckling to myself and munching on a bag of corn nuts as I cruise home along Highway 13.

There's no feeling in my legs.

By the way, Culver's had a cookie dough special, so I grabbed a small cone on the way out of town.

I finished off the last of the Milk Duds as I pulled into the garage, still pondering the low metabolism that's making me gain weight.

I just can't understand it!

It's a mystery.

Needing to give this further thought, I tromp though the house, grab a licorice stick off the counter and head for the sauna.

Now...I will confess that the thought of a 300-pounder sitting naked in the sauna isn't pretty, but it's a quiet, relaxing, place to think.

This weight thing has me baffled.

I'm sweating like a cold Pepsi on a hot afternoon when it suddenly hits me.

I jump up and, in my excitement, charge out of the sauna for the house.

Now...that may have been a mistake.

We have neighbors.

So...I run back to the sauna, grab a towel, actually two towels, to cover myself and charge into the kitchen.

Thinking the sauna is on fire, Laurie screams.

"Relax," I squealed, "I've got the answer!"

"It's water retention!"

"The body is 90-percent water......so I only weigh 30 pounds!!!"

With a smirk and raised eyebrow, I hit her with the money question: "What's for dinner?"

Play Ball!

PLAY BALL!

It's been a big week here in Port Wing, as the village got ready for the home opener of the town team baseball club.

The excitement was building the entire week.

It was all the talk at Johnson's store.

Up here on the North end, we worried about color coordination of the uniforms.

Down at the bank, they were speculating on a name for the club.

Ichabod threw out the "Coho's," but he was just fishing….no one took the bait.

Still didn't have a name for the club when the boys took the field on Sunday.

Game time temperature was 68-degrees.

The smell of brats and burgers was in the air, the stands were packed with friends and neighbors visiting during the pre-game warm-up, Big Jim was "taping up" and getting his umpire gear ready.

This is baseball the way it's meant to be played, afternoon game, wood bats, local field, young men playing just for the joy of playing baseball.

We haven't won a game in 35 years.

The last time Port Wing won a game in the Upper 13 league was in 1971.

Bing Anderson was the manager of the team at the time.

Bing was on hand Sunday afternoon to throw out the first ball.

He's in his 80's now, but he still has an arm…..brought the heater with his ceremonial first pitch.

Moose did the honors for the National Anthem…..acapella.

I gave him a hug after his performance.

It has never been done better at any major league ball park.

It was a special afternoon.

We had a bit of a challenge getting ready for the season this year.

When the boys went upstairs to open up the press box, earlier in the week, they found a family of raccoons had established residency and were in no mood to vacate the premises.

Unfortunately, none of us speak raccoon, so it was difficult communicating with mama to insure her that we meant no harm.

Turns out none of the boys really wanted to take on a grumpy mama raccoon with babies anyway, so it was a stand off.

Mama raccoon finally got bored and waddled down the left field line, leaving the kids standing by the pop cooler.

The boys bundled up the little buggers in a box and followed mama, who was waiting for us 325 feet down the left field line, right at the foul pole.

We got the message.

She felt she and her family had been fouled, but it turns out they're quite happy in their new home, just beyond the left field fence.

Couple of the boys made it a point to visit them just before game time on Sunday to make sure everything was working out well for the family.

Mama raccoon and the kids were quite comfortable, sitting in lawn chairs with a cool drink, shades, and a box of popcorn.

It's tough to find lawn chairs that size, but they fit like a glove.

I think Joey found them in Iron River at a garage sale.

Promptly at 1:30, we heard Big Jim yell: "Play ball!"

What a day!

Up in the press box we had a few glitches, probably due to opening day jitters.

We started the day by testing the load limit on the ladder when I went scrambling up the stairs.

No cracks, no breaks…..must be good northern Wisconsin pine in that ladder.

Bottom of the 5th, a spider was crawling up my leg and I missed an out as I'm frantically trying to find it.

I thought it was a tick.

Caught him, just above the knee……the spider.

Went into a full wind-up when I flung that spider out of the press box, but her web caught on my finger and she came snapping back into my face like a Nolan Ryan fastball.

Tested the load limit on the ladder again trying to get away from that spider, but we both calmed right down when we spotted fresh buns and brats.

Fortunately, I speak spider, so we wound up sharing a brat and a cup of coffee before I found her a new home.

Turns out she had been living in the press box with the raccoons since 1985.

It was that kind of day.

Ichabod kept trying to hang up the runs on the scoreboard between innings, but most of the hooks were missing. We had to skip a few innings.

Seems to me we were missing a few numbers too, so if you looked at the scoreboard from the bleachers, it was only an estimate.

Little work needed in that area next week.

The press box is right above the concession stand.

We caught Carpo lining up for a brat and just about changed his nickname to Lefty when we dropped one of the scoreboard signs, but he was too quick for us and got out of the way in time.

Ichabod got a little confused in the top of the 9th, when he thought the game was over.

He thanked everyone for coming, told them to be careful driving home, and then found out that our boys still had an at-bat left in the game.

Ichabod was mumbling something about a talking spider, but he covered nicely.

"OK," he growled, "everybody hold it. The game isn't over yet, everyone back to their seats."

Must have been some authority in that statement...everyone sat down.

We maintained a full house to the end.

It was a wonderful afternoon.

Cost of admission: 0

An afternoon with friends, spiders, raccoons, and neighbors: Priceless

We're looking forward to the next home stand.
Oh….by the way….we lost the opener.
Final score: Ashland 16   Port Wing 6
Beautiful!
The streak is still alive!!

The Warrior

THE WARRIOR

The Warrior enters the building.
His full beard is black and shaggy.
Long, black, hair flows well past his shoulders.
He wears eyeglasses from the sixties.... heavy, black, frames with thick lenses.
A man in his mid-fifties, he carries no more than 150 pounds on a frame that is well over six feet.
He shuffles along, head down, hanging onto the arm of an elderly, white-haired, woman.
The Warrior and his mother are in the basement of a church in Ashland, Wisconsin.
It is Christmas day.
They are here for Christmas dinner, served by a wonderful group of volunteers.
The Warrior wears dirty jeans, tennis shoes, a short sleeve, khaki, military shirt, and a military fatigue jacket with the sleeves cut off. The rank insignia on his shirt is that of a Marine.
His fatigue jacket has four ribbons above the left pocket.
As he steps in front of me for gravy on his potatoes, I say: "We've got a Veteran here. Merry Christmas!"
The Warrior doesn't look up.
The mother looks at her son and smiles.
I watch as he and his mother sit down, two lonely figures at the far end of a long table.
The Warrior eats quickly, shoveling food into his mouth with his left hand, never looking up.
His mother watches him, leaving her food untouched.
She seems far away.
She reaches across the table and touches his hair.
The Warrior doesn't look up.
When he finishes his meal, the Warrior abruptly stands, picks up his plate, and shuffles to the front of the room, eyes locked on the floor.
Leaving his plate with the dirty dishes, he shuffles back to the serving line, grabs a fresh plate, and comes through for a second meal.

When he reaches my gravy station, I say: "It's cold out there. Good to see you getting a hot meal, brother. Thanks for making a sacrifice for us."

The Warrior hesitates a moment, then turns and shuffles, head down, back to his table.

His mother watches him with a sad, half-smile, tugging at her lips.

It appears that she isn't sure if she wants to laugh or cry.

She quietly watches the Warrior as he begins the routine again, quickly shoveling food into his mouth with his left hand, eyes glued to the table.

Her meal is still untouched.

When he finishes, the Warrior places his fork on his plate, folds his hands in his lap, and sits quietly, head down.

His mother reaches over to touch his arm, then leans across the table and whispers in his ear.

He nods his head, then grabs his mothers arm as she escorts him to the front of the room.

Surprisingly, they come to me.

She starts to hand me several bills, then says: "My son would like to pay for his meals."

It takes a few moments to collect myself before I'm able to speak.

When I'm able to pull myself together, I respond with: "He already did. A long time ago. We are grateful."

I recognized one of the ribbons on his chest the first time he came through the serving line.

The red center, flanked by white and blue, identifies the combat medal as a Silver Star, awarded for gallantry in action.

It is third in line behind the Congressional Medal of Honor and the Distinguished Service Cross.

This Marine, indeed, is a Warrior.

I look at the Warrior with tears in my eyes.

He raises his head, smiles, and gives me the peace sign.

I flash the peace sign back and quietly reply: "Semper Fi."

The Warrior smiles, nods his head, then walks out of the church, head up, escorting his mother.

This time, it is she who is holding onto the arm of her son.

Today is a good day.

Merry Christmas.

WHERE ARE THE HEROES?

A while back, I listened to a speaker pound away at this theme, "America has lost its heroes."

Not a chance!

I get very weary of the pompous windbags who spew this pabulum and the people who believe it.

I got up and left the room.

If we have lost anything as Americans, it is our perspective, our picture, of a hero.

Our memory is short, so I'm not surprised.

How quickly we have forgotten 9-11 and the chilling pictures of New York firemen charging into a doomed World Trade Tower.

Do you think they may have been terrified?

Did it slow them down?

Not a step!

That same courage and commitment is shown every day across the country when our volunteer firemen and emergency response personnel pull on their turnout gear and head for another emergency, putting our safety and welfare ahead of their own.

America hasn't lost its heroes, it's forgotten where to look for them…. AGAIN!

The American Hero doesn't drive a race car, dance in the end zone, or throw a baseball 98 miles an hour.

The American Hero doesn't slam dunk a basketball, slap a hockey puck or kick a soccer ball.

The American Hero doesn't throw a football 60 yards or sing a rock song.

The American Hero gets up and goes to work every morning in order to feed a family and pay a mortgage.

The American Hero is in a manufacturing plant, a grocery store, an office building, a patrol car, an ambulance, and a fire engine.

The American Hero is in a school, a hospital, and a shopping mall.

The American Hero wears a Kevlar helmet and defends our country.

The American Hero is the electrician, the plumber, the carpenter, and the truck driver.

They're in Port Wing and Paducah, Cornucopia and Casper, Iron River and Iron Mountain.

They're in Poplar and Pittsburgh……Ashland and Anaheim…..Mason and Missoula.

They're in every small village, town, and city across this country.

The American Hero is……….YOU!

It's time we put the true picture of our American Heroes back on the wall.

My Uncle Lester was a railroader.

He was just a kid in 1945, fresh out of the army after serving our country in WWII, when he hooked up with the railroad.

Lester thought he'd give it a try for a summer.

He stayed 42 years.

Lester worked from the bottom up….. not many people willing to do that anymore.

His first job was pounding spikes for the Great Northern railroad.

It was backbreaking work.

Lester worked on track used by the Empire Builder in a time when that big steamer rumbled through my home town at six o'clock every night, right on the dot.

I would stand by Grote's gas station, wide eyed, as the ground started to shake and the monster came snarling into town belching thick, black, smoke.

The engineer started sounding the whistle a mile out of town.

Sometimes he'd wave to the kid by the gas station.

I never tired of the sight of this massive steel horse hissing and whistling through town.

I thought the Empire Builder would rumble through town forever, every night at six o'clock, on the dot.

That engineer was my hero.

I wanted to drive the Empire Builder when I grew up, but the monster disappeared over the years, replaced by new, more efficient, engines.

Time moves on….things change…. so do our heroes.

As I grew up, I would play checkers with Uncle Lester on the weekends and talk about steam locomotives.

Sometimes I'd win, but most often, Lester would win.

He'd say: "Don't expect me to let you win. Ya gotta earn it. Life isn't a free ride."

I miss them both, Lester and the checker games.

We could only play checkers on the weekends.

Lester was on a bridge crew.

He would leave home at two or three o'clock on Monday morning and return Friday evening.

For most of his career he lived during the week in a boxcar converted to a bunkhouse and ate his meals in a cook car.

42 years!

I'm sure you could count on one hand the number of days Lester missed work in that 42 year time frame.

He wasn't happy every day and he didn't love his job every day, matter of fact, I would guess there were many days that he hated his job, when the winter wind whistled across the prairie, but he was there because his crew counted on him to be there.

The railroad counted on him to be there.

He didn't complain, he didn't whine.

Lester wasn't working for a paycheck, he was working for the railroad.

I can remember only one time that Lester raised his voice.

I made the mistake of slipping out of work early and showing up at his house.

He knew I was supposed to be on the job.

That day, a young kid with all the answers got a little advice from his uncle.

He looked at me and grumbled: "If you're getting paid for eight hours, give them eight hours. That doesn't mean sitting on your ass for two hours and expecting to be paid for it. I thought you were better than that!"

I was embarrassed, but the point was made.

A full days work for a full days pay.

I have tried to follow that advice for my entire adult life and pass it along to my children.

For 42 years, Lester showed me the traits of an American Hero.

1. Loyalty
2. Dependability
3. 100% effort
4. Respect for co-workers and Company.
5. No whining.
6. A full day for full pay.

Has America lost its heroes?
No.

We're just looking in the wrong place…..AGAIN!

Look around and you'll quickly be able to identify an American Hero.

It's the average person trying to make a living and be a role model for the family…..day after day…..year after year…..just like my Uncle Lester……just like you.

Take a bow…..it's about time you were recognized!

ROLE MODEL

We're a proud bunch in Port Wing today.

One of our own has done well....REAL WELL!!

On February 20, 2008, with eight minutes and fifty-two seconds left in the ball game, Port Wing's Jolene Anderson, who dreamed of being a Wisconsin Badger since she was a little girl, hit a 15-foot jump shot at the Kohl Center, in front of a home crowd, and became the all-time leading scorer in the history of University of Wisconsin basketball, and that includes the men's program.

With 2218 points hammered through the net in her Badger career, Jolene surpassed Alando Tucker, who previously held the record.

It should be noted here that Jolene set the record in 118 games, compared to 135 games for Alando.

The net was still jiggling when a quick time-out was called, allowing the crowd to give Jolene a standing ovation.

There was no chest thumping and waving of arms by Jolene.

A television shot showed her calmly walking to the Badger bench, looking up at the ceiling, and then glancing at her family.

No hysterics.

That IS Jolene Anderson.

An emotional television shot showed her mother, Julie, wiping a tear from her eye.

Julie may have been remembering the endless thump....thump....thump of a basketball echoing off the walls of a barn on the family farm as Jolene was growing up and practicing that jump shot hour after hour, even when the winter winds were whistling through the cracks in the walls.

Julie may have been thinking of the career (2881 pts)....single game (58) and single season (956) scoring records that Jolene still holds in Wisconsin High School basketball.

Julie may have been thinking of her mother, Jolene's grandmother, who recently passed away, as Jolene may have done when she looked at the ceiling of the Kohl Center.

Julie may have been thinking of the answer Jolene listed in her biography when asked: "Who inspired you the most in basketball?" She answered: "My mom."

I won't ask them what they were thinking, because their thoughts should be private.

More likely, Julie was just very proud of her daughter.

The headlines of that record-setting game will highlight the 15-foot jumper that put Jolene into the record books, but I think an equally important play occurred a few minutes earlier, a play that identifies the character of this remarkable young woman.

Jolene had a breakaway steal and a clear path to a "bunny" lay-up that would have put her into the record books, but she unselfishly passed the ball to a teammate, who scored the easy basket.

That is typical of Jolene's values…..team first.

Just a short time later, that same teammate fired a bullet to Jolene on the baseline and she broke the record.

Jolene's line for the record-breaking night will show 18 points….10 rebounds and three assists.

A double-double……but the three assists, the one in particular, speaks volumes to the character of this humble young woman who started her basketball career in a barn.

Her values come from her parents and she confirms that in her biography with an answer to the question of: "Who are the persons you most admire?"

Her answer: "My parents."

The media will chronicle the points scored, but they don't chronicle the throng of young kids clustered around Jolene after every game, and they don't mention how she patiently takes the time to sign an autograph for each of them.

The media doesn't see what happens in her home town of Port Wing, a tiny village of only 500 people on the shore of Lake Superior, when a car stops at Johnson's Store to ask for directions to Jolene Anderson's home.

They want to see the barn.

The media doesn't see the admiration her home town has for this young woman, an ordinary woman who has accomplished extraordinary things.

Jolene owns more Wisconsin Badger basketball records than I could possibly mention here.

She has earned three gold medals as a member of USA National basketball teams.

She has earned the admiration of everyone she meets, through her conduct, her accomplishments, and her integrity.

By the way, lest anyone think Jolene is nothing more than a scoring machine for the Badgers, I took a few moments to research where

Jolene ranks in the various marks recorded each year in the Big Ten Conference.

As this column is being written, here is where Jolene ranks in the Big Ten.

Scoring	# 1
Minutes played	# 1
Assist/Turnover ratio	# 1
Free throw percent	# 3
Offensive rebounds	# 3
Rebounding	# 4
3-Point FG made	# 4
ASSISTS	# 6
Defensive rebounds	# 6
3-point percent	# 8

In ten (10) separate categories, Jolene ranks among the Top Ten players in the Big Ten Conference and she is the Number One player in three (3) separate categories.

That ain't bad for a kid who learned how to play basketball in a barn.

Jolene Anderson can be described in just two words: ROLE MODEL!

There aren't many. That's what makes her so special.

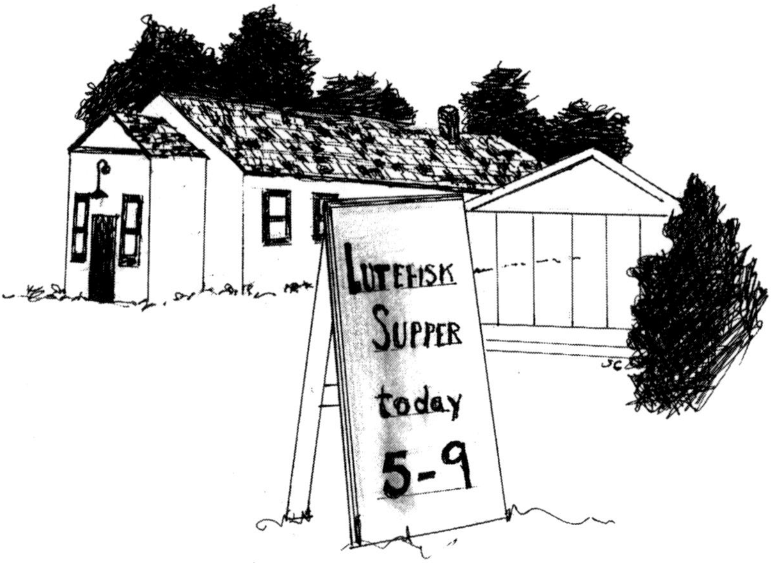
LUTEFISK
SUPPER
today
5-9

LUTEFISK SEASON

We're getting ready for the annual Lutefisk Festival up here in northern Wisconsin.

The Lutherans usually set the pace.

The churches are laying in big supplies of cod and lye, industrial strength cleaner is purchased to clean the plates after dinner and the local EMS crews are on alert.

The Port Wing town hall is brightly lit every night.

The ladies are already working on side dishes of meatballs and gravy, mashed rutabaga, green pea stew, and potatoes.

The desserts are always decadent.

Of course, you must have lefse in large quantities.

I love lefse.

Actually, I love lefse, bacon, meatballs and gravy, mashed rutabaga, green pea stew and potatoes, but try as I might over the years, I can't handle lutefisk.

It tastes like soap, it smells, and quite frankly, it scares me.

Essentially, lutefisk is a chemically treated white fish that can also be used as a drain cleaner.

I heard one of the Swedes up here lost a hand when he was soaking lutefisk in lye, but no one has ever confirmed that it actually happened.

The Finlanders call it lipeakala, but it's still lutefisk.

A couple of Finlanders tried to slip one by me when I first moved up here.

In retrospect, I suppose it could have been retaliation.

My wife, Laurie, had been teaching me what she SAID, what she SAID, was a cheery Finnish greeting.

So, attending my first Lutefisk Festival with the locals at the town hall, we sat down with a couple of distinguished looking gentlemen.

While we were visiting, I found out they were Finnish, so I passed along Laurie's cheery greeting.

"Hiesta Mina Nupa!"

I gave the boys a big smile.

Laurie looked like a deer caught in the headlights.

I thought someone had passed gas.

Apparently, roughly translated, this means: "Smell my bellybutton."

The Finlanders were talking among themselves after I committed this faux pas.

As soon as I looked away, they camouflaged a couple large chunks of lutefisk under my potatoes.

Brought me to my knees.

Knocked out my taste buds for months!

Fortunately, Hjalmar Hiekkalinna was there to hose me down.

I'm a little fuzzy on that, but I think it was a guy named Hjalmar.

It was all a blur.

After the incident, I would break out in a cold sweat every time anyone said: "Just try a little bit."

I'm in a cold sweat right now, as a matter of fact, just typing those words.

I feel like a survivor after I've "tried a little bit" of lutefisk.

Here's a bit of background on the care and handling of lutefisk, from the sea to the serving.

First, you soak the fish for five to six days in cold water, changing the water each day.

Then it's soaked in a solution of cold water and lye for two more days.

By now, the fish is like jelly, it's full of lye and it is POISONOUS!

Oh baby!

Keep it away from the kids.

Before you can eat this bad boy, there are another four to six days and nights of soaking in cold water.

Again, the water must be changed every day.

You've got two weeks invested in this cowboy before it's ready for the oven.

We don't give our dogs that much attention.

Here's the kicker, once you get 'er cooked and served, ya gotta move quick in cleaning those dishes.

If you don't clean the lutefisk off pots, pans, plates, spoons, knives, and forks right away, you'll need a quarter stick of dynamite to break it loose.

This gives "sticks to your ribs" a whole new meaning.

I tell you what, you either love it or hate it.

Most people up in this part of the country know Mike Granlund.

Mike is a native of the area and a former star athlete at South Shore High; I think they called him "The Flying Finn."

Mike is also active as a sports broadcaster on local radio stations, which adds to his notoriety in northwestern Wisconsin.

He seems to know everyone in a ten-county area and is a font of information on local history.

Mike loves to visit.

Couple months ago, Mike invited me out "ta home" for lefse, but his directions left my head spinning.

He routed me to the Finlander Freeway, double-F, then had me jumping off on O, the Oulu off-ramp.

It was a mess.

I wound up over by Ticklebelly Hill, asking a guy named Ino, who lived somewhere on the Minnesota North Shore, how to get back to I-13.

He said: "I tink it's 'bout tree miles behind ya. Yust turn 'er around ta da nort' and you'll run right into 'er. 'Bout tree miles, I tink. Ya becha."

Nice man.

I thanked him kindly and moved on, but I never did find the house, so I missed out on the lefse buffet.

Anyway, Mike tells me the story of an 81-year-old woman who was entering a church hall over by Oulu during the lutefisk season.

Lutheran church, as I recall.

The poor lady fell and broke her hip, but she would not allow the EMS personnel to take her to the hospital until she had her lutefisk.

I wouldn't doubt she threw away her cane and jogged part of the way.

Lutefisk will do that to you.

This lady definitely is in the "love it" camp.

Actually, I think it's required that Finlanders, Swedes, and Norwegians be in the "love it" camp, but here again, nothing I can confirm.

Hjalmar Hiekkalinna could probably give me the facts on this, but I'm still not sure if he's a real person.

As I recall it, Tuija Tiirikka was throwing the Heimlech on me during the aforementioned "incident" at the town hall, while Hjalmar was hosing me down, but it's pretty foggy.

Could be neither of them exist and I was hallucinating from the lye.

Secretly, I wonder if even the Swedes, Finns, and Norwegians eat lutefisk more than once a year.

Personally, I would rather pass a kidney stone.

Ya becha!

NO MORE YESTERDAYS

How many of us would like to re-live yesterday?

In today's lightening-fast world of cell phones, instant communication, five-year business plans, and corporate demand to do more with less, the pundits tell us that yesterday is living in the past, that only the future is important.

Yesterday does matter.

If you could go back to yesterday, would you change anything?

Would you bury a grudge, make a phone call, or stop by to see an old friend?

If you knew it was your last chance, is there anything you would like to say to your spouse, parents, brothers, sisters, or friends?

There's no guarantee of tomorrow.

Every year, in early summer, I'm reminded of a beautiful June morning in 1982.

A heavy dew was on the grass, the bird's were singing a lively tune in the trees, and the crickets were still chirping a summer symphony as a young couple left the country home they loved so much to begin the first day of a new career.

They were enroute to an event some two hundred miles away, but they enjoyed each other's company, so the time and miles passed quickly.

After they arrived, the young woman was visiting with a friend across the room.

She stood up, said she felt dizzy, then collapsed.

The young man raced across the room to find his companion lying face up on the floor.

He grabbed her hand.

It was cold.

He looked into her eyes, but received only an empty stare in return.

"What happened here?"

"I don't know," came the reply. "She said she felt dizzy, then she collapsed."

The young man looked at the faces staring at him.

"Will someone please call an ambulance.........NOW!!!"

It seemed a simple request, but no one had taken the initiative to get help for what was obviously a life-threatening situation.

As the call went out for an ambulance, the woman went into convulsions.

The young man didn't know what to do, so he held her tight and talked to her until the paramedics arrived.

She didn't hear.

When the paramedics arrived, the young man wouldn't let go.

They gently pulled him away.

Paramedics began asking the young woman to give them her name, then yelled at her in an effort to get a response.

There was none.

She took a shuddering breath, then another.

The paramedics were no longer trying to mask their concern.

A high-speed trip to a local hospital left her in the emergency room, where a doctor quickly began an examination.

He looked at the frightened young man and said: "I need to ask you some questions."

"Of course," came the response.

"Is she taking any kind of drugs?" the doctor asked.

"No," came the response. "She is addicted to drugs and alcohol, but she has been clean and sober for five years."

"May I look in her purse?" the doctor questioned.

"Certainly, anything that may help," came a quick reply from the young man, who kept staring at the unconscious woman on the examining table.

A search of the purse revealed a bottle of aspirin.

"Has anyone ever told her she has cancer?" the doctor asked.

"Cancer?" the young man stared incredulously at the doctor. "Why in hell would anyone tell her she has cancer?"

"Please calm down," the doctor replied. "She has a multi-colored mole on her left hip that looks suspicious."

"No," came back the response from the deflated young man, "No one has ever told her she has cancer."

The doctor spoke again, "I suspect it is an aneurysm. I've detected a build-up of blood behind the right eye, but we don't have the equipment to treat it in this hospital. She will have to be transported to a metropolitan trauma center."

Now a terrified young man asked the question: "What are her chances?"

The doctor seemed to have difficultly himself as he put his arm around the husband and said: "At best...50-50. The pneumonia will be a problem."

The one-hour trip to the trauma center seemed like it took days.

A young woman doctor came into the waiting room after another examination had been completed.

"We have just completed a CAT scan and it shows a major bleed on the right side of her head."

The young man had a question: "What does that mean in layman's terminology?"

The doctor reached out to take his hand.

"It means she is very critical."

The young man felt like his throat was closing, shutting off his ability to breathe.

The doctor called for a nearby nurse and whispered instructions.

Within seconds, the nurse appeared with a paper bag.

"You're hyperventilating," said the doctor. "Put this over your nose and mouth, then breathe, slowly. You'll be all right."

When the young man recovered, he said: "Is there a Catholic priest in the hospital? If there is a possibility we are going to lose her, she must have last rites."

The doctor squeezed the young man's hand.

"I'll show you to the chapel, then notify a priest."

Once in the chapel, the young man stood in front of a statue of Christ, arms extended.

"Why are you testing me again?" he asked in a low voice. "Didn't I pass the test with the drug addiction and the alcohol? Why did you give her back to us if you're going to take her away again? What have I done to anger you?"

He was the only one in the chapel and the young man knew, even in his grief, it was silly to be angry with God.

He kneeled, then began to pray silently to himself.

"I know in my heart that this is part of the plan you have for me. I don't know why you're testing me again, but I will do as you wish. If you are to take her, give me the courage to be strong enough to carry on and raise our children. If you'll take a trade, I will go instead of her."

The young man was startled when he felt a hand on his shoulder.

"I'm Father Murphy. I've been to the intensive care unit. Your wife has received the last rites of the Catholic Church. What can I do to help you?"

"I don't know Father, unless you have a direct line to the boss."

The priest smiled and replied: "We all do. There's always an operator on duty. Looks like you're on the line now."

The priest walked up several flights of stairs with the young man.

When they reached the intensive care unit, they were ushered into a small, windowless, room.

A neurosurgeon stepped into the room.

"You can see her now."

The doctor made the statement matter of fact, as though they were going to see a used car.

As the two walked into the intensive care room, they young man began to see shooting stars and have difficulty breathing again.

How could this be happening?

It was only a few hours ago that this beautiful woman was smiling and joking with her children.

She called her mother: "We're leaving now Mom. I love you. See you Monday."

Ten hours later, she's lying in this sterile hospital room, with tubes attached to all parts of her body, oblivious to her surroundings.

She's only 32 years old.

How can this happen?

The young man held her hand and sat alone with his thoughts, wondering how he would break the news to their children and her mother.

Yesterday was a great day, we were planting flowers by the deck.

If only we could turn back the clock.

The sun was beginning to set as the young woman's two children and her mother arrived at the hospital.

"How is she?" asked the mother.

"It's not good," the young man replied. "She is very critical. We have to face the fact that she may die."

"No!" The mother yelled, "No! She is not going to die! She is not going to die! I want to see her!"

The mother began crying when she stepped into her daughter's room.

She walked over to the side of the bed and took her hand.

It was cold.

"Oh, honey," she said over and over again. "Oh, honey."

She laid her head on her daughter's chest and began to sob.

A short time later the neurosurgeon came back into the room and told us the young woman had passed away.

She was 32 years old.

You don't die when you're 32 years old, leaving a five and seven-year-old daughter.

Yesterday she felt fine.

Yesterday we were planting flowers.

I must apologize for using a rather lengthy life story to illustrate this point.

We all spend a lot of time wishing for things we don't have and not nearly enough time being thankful for, and fully appreciating, those things in life that really matter, priceless moments with each other.

In the final analysis, is there anything else that matters?

When we reach the end of our life's journey, we will remember only the moments and events that left us breathless.

Watching the fog roll in off the big water or the Northern Lights dancing their way across the Northern sky with someone you love……..or planting flowers.

Don't miss any of these moments.

Today will be yesterday tomorrow.

Make today a good day.

If you have tomorrow, it's a bonus.

Butter Pecan

BUTTER PECAN

"I don't remember her very much, unless I see pictures."
She was five when her mother died.
The memories have faded away.
It was a sunny day, one of those summer afternoon's when the smell of fresh mown hay is in the air.
June 12th.
Her mother said she felt dizzy, tried to stand up, and then collapsed.
She was gone.
A massive cerebral hemorrhage.
The shock is unimaginable.
She was only 32 years old.
"You know, I didn't even have time to say good-bye to your mother. I ran across the room and grabbed her hand, but she was gone."
The daughter looked at her father.
She could feel the sadness.
"You never talk about that day," she said.
"It was a bad day," her father quietly replied.
The daughter picked up another picture, this one of her and her mother at an amusement park.
"Someday you'll feel like talking about it, dad."
Her father stared out the window.
The pain was buried for a long time.
The day after his daughter's mother died, he was attending mass with her and her sister.
The father started crying when the priest announced the death of his wife and their mother.
The oldest daughter, then seven years old, grabbed his hand and said: "Dad, don't cry! When you cry I can hardly breathe!"
He didn't cry anymore.
The tears were buried deep within the pain for nearly a year....until Mother's Day.
With his two daughters in tow, the father visited his wife's grave for the first time.
When he saw her name on the gravestone, he sank to his knees and began to cry uncontrollably.

He stayed there for a long time, kneeling in front of the gravestone, his hand on her name, unleashing months of grief, unaware of his daughter's presence.

When the pent up grief was spent, he rose, took his daughters by the hand and left the cemetery.

He didn't return.

There was little talk of their mother after that day.

No doubt, his daughters wanted to talk about her, but they were likely afraid dad would fall apart again, like he did at the grave.

It wasn't fair to them.

As his mind came back to the present, his daughter was looking at another picture of her mother.

"I really don't know anything about her.

I don't know how she talked or what she liked to wear.

I don't know what we did together, what made her laugh, or what made her cry.

I don't even know if she liked ice cream."

The father could see frustration in his daughter as she continued to sift through the old family pictures.

It happened a long time ago.

The five-year-old child is now a 25-year-old woman.

Where had the time gone?

Her father had always planned to tell her and her sister about their mother, but the time had slipped away.

The pain was too deep.

The memories stayed buried deep inside.

When is the right time?

When do the memories fade away?

Each of the pictures has a story, but they need a storyteller.

Is there time to tell all the stories, to pass them along to another storyteller?

How do we know if there will be another day?

There wasn't on June 12th.

Where do we begin?

Her father continued to stare out the window, watching the Arizona sun set on another Memorial Day.

Memorial Day!!!

How fitting!

The father turned his gaze to his daughter.

"Butter pecan," he said.

"What?"

A puzzled look from his daughter.

"Butter pecan," came the reply.

"Your mother liked butter pecan ice cream."

THE BAGPIPER AND THE GUNS

I have a problem with death.

I don't handle it well.

It is one of my many character flaws.

This morning, what began as another great day turned dark, when I returned home to find a message on our answering machine.

It was from the daughter of a friend.

Her father, who was a neighbor and good friend for many years, had died the previous evening of a massive heart attack.

Curt was 59 years old.

How quickly our lives can change.

The end can arrive like a bolt of lightening.

I wonder if we all have an appreciation for every day of life, or do we tend to take things for granted all too often?

I would suspect the latter.

I try to live every day like it's my last, but I leave a lot of gaps.

In all likelihood, most of us do.

If you were to be informed today that this is your last day on earth, what would you do?

How would you spend your final day?

Would you write a letter to your spouse and your children?

Would you write a letter to your grandchildren?

Who would you call, and more importantly, what would you say?

How many times, and to how many people, would you say: "I love you"?

Is there someone who has made a difference in your life?

Have you said "thank you"?

Would you let go of that grudge you've carried for years?

Would you have love in your heart on your final day, or would you be vindictive, and tell those jerks who have haunted you all these years how you really feel about them?

I would think most of us would enter the final lap with love in our hearts.

As I sit here this evening, I'm thinking of Mary, Curt's wife, and the grief she feels tonight, a grief that actually has physical pain.

I have felt that pain in my lifetime.

It is unbearable.

Perhaps that's why I struggle so much with those who have suffered loss.

My emotions come to the surface too quickly.

My throat seems to close…the words won't come.

It's a cheap excuse to erase my guilt.

It took me two years to finally get out the words to a friend who lost a daughter.

I felt so bad for his loss and shed many tears, privately, during those two years, but he didn't know it.

I couldn't find the words.

Two years!

We search so hard to find the right words to describe our feelings during these terrible times, when a simple: "I'm sorry for your loss" is more often than not the most comforting words.

So, we will be attending another funeral, saluting the life of a friend…. and a soldier.

Curt was part of the brotherhood, a brotherhood comprised of those of us who have served our country.

We were soldiers…and airmen…and marines…and sailors.

We were there when the country needed us.

Frequently, at these events, we stare off into the distance, alone with our thoughts, as a bagpiper plays "Amazing Grace."

Our eyes mist over when the mournful sound of "Taps" echoes across the countryside.

We flinch at the first volley of a 21-gun salute, then steel ourselves as the bolts slam another round into the rifles, and the commander orders: "Fire!"

Another round into the chamber, and again the commander orders: "Fire!"

We stand a little taller when the third round slams into the breech and the order comes to: "Fire!"

The 21-gun salute always sends shivers up my spine.

It always draws tears from deep within the well of my emotions.

I would guess that most of us, those of us in the brotherhood, want the guns when it is our time.

It is the final show of respect to a fallen veteran of the military.

I most often refer to a funeral as a celebration of life, rather than a sad affair, but I'm having a hard time with the death of my friend, Curt.

The suddenness of it all has hit me like a fist in the chest.

I suppose I think about these things more now, since I am closer to the end of my life than I am to the beginning.

I must admit that I wonder, from time to time, when the bagpiper will play for me.

I don't want to know in advance when that day will come, but when it does.....I want the guns.

For now, those selfish thoughts of my own final call will have to drift far into the background.

There is something much more important we have to deal with on this day.

The bagpiper is waiting for my friend, Curt.

So are the guns.

At the Hop . . . . . . at 60!

AT THE HOP......AT 60!

Those of you in your 20's or early 30's will have no idea what we're talking about when the "seasoned citizens" of my era talk about a Sock Hop.

They were somethin'!

These social mixers of the 50's and 60's began on a Friday night, after a football or basketball game, when nose-pickin', head hangin', red-faced guys in the sophomore and junior classes of the local high school lined up on one side of the gym, while the young ladies of the same class level lined up on the other side of the gym, sizing up the dance prospects.

The seniors were out in the parking lot with a six-pack or up on Blueberry Hill.

I never did get there, although I spent my entire high school career trying to convince one of the ladies to accompany me up the hill.

The response was always something like: "When pigs fly!"

You can't imagine how much I hoped for pork in the air during those years.

I had a ten-page list of chicks, with phone numbers, who gave me the pig response during my high school tenure.

I was ready for high flyin' hogs!

Never made a call!

Anyway, back at the dance, the shoes were off, hence the "sock hop," and one of the locals was crankin' out the tunes from a stack of 45's that stood ready for action like pancakes drippin' syrup at the International House of Pancakes.

When that first 45 fired up, usually a toe tapper like the Stones or the Beatles, the action, or inaction, got started.

There were normally a couple studs at these dances, with a pack of Lucky Strikes rolled up in the sleeve of a t-shirt, who would be off like a shot to the best looking babes in the gym.

They always scored a dance.

I still don't know how they did it.

The rest of us would stand around, head down, pickin' our nose, kickin' at the gym floor, hoping one of the ladies would take pity on us and ask us to dance.

They rarely did.

Matter of fact, in my case, they never did!

Might have been that nose pickin'.

We would have done the asking, you understand, but there was always the possibility that the girl would say no, leaving us mortified.

When that happened, there was no way out.

The fellas lined up on the other side of the gym knew you got the "no-go," meaning you had to walk the gauntlet, taking a pounding from the boys as you limped back to your side of the gym.

That's probably the reason I never attended a prom, the possibility of being turned down.

Course, they would never tell me where the prom was being held, and the one year they did tell me, turned out it was the week before. I might also mention that the location they gave me was suspect.

I show up for the prom, at the address they gave me, and found out it was an auction barn.

You don't see many guys going to a livestock auction in a formal white jacket, with a red cumberbund.

Humiliating!

I bought two chickens and a duck, just to let them know I meant to be there.

But, I digress.

Now at some point in the evening, that first slow dance fired up.

Oh baby!

The geeks on the far side of the gym, me among them, had been firing each other up all night for that first slow dance.

"I'm gonna ask Diane."

Oh man, if I could have just ONE dance with Diane.

We always geared up for the hottest babe at the dance.

Fat chance!

Elvis would have showed up at that dance before Diane would have danced with one of us.

Course, we never did ask, so who knows?

We sat out the slow dances, and the fast ones, pretending we didn't care, while we were crying inside.

End of the night, we left the dance, took a few extra minutes to "drag main," then headed for home, defeated again.

The studs had all the luck.

Those dances seemed so important back then.

Well, now that we're sixty, I like to imagine what would happen if we returned for another "sock hop," more than forty years later.

Could it be that we did return?

The studs are still there, but instead of a pack of Luckies rolled up in their sleeves, they have a sampler pack of Viagra.

One dude, who had cornered the market on Brylcreem forty years ago, has three stands of hair left.

They're a foot long and combed side to side…from ear to ear.

When the wind catches them….they flare out like a wind sock.

Man, the seniors are really senior now.

The dudes who used to be out in the parking lot drinking beer are still there, but now they're slamming Metamucil and comparing the medication they're taking for various ailments.

They just want to be regular guys these days.

The dudes who used to score a dance every time they asked were still game, but they lost interest after dragging that oxygen tank across the room a few times.

Laurie took pity on me and said, after all these years, that she would go with me to Blueberry Hill.

Be still my heart!

I "floored it" and "squealed out" toward the Hill.

Blueberry Hill is now a condo development.

Laurie and I cruised through there, just so I could say I made it to Blueberry Hill…45 years late.

And you know what?

Just as we were leaving, I looked up and saw a kid flying a kite that had the form of a pig.

Damn, I guess pigs do fly!

Back at the dance, the dude who turned all the ladies heads with a jacked-up, "primo," '57 Chevy in 1961 is still driving that '57 Chevy.

Paint has faded a little; those fuzzy dice are still hanging from the mirror.

They look pretty ragged.

"Snorkey" is still a handsome devil, but he's been divorced three times and never held a job for more than a year.

"Snork" walked up to a group of ladies and gave them his best line: "How you doin'?"

"Apparently better than you," comes the reply.

Guess life didn't work out as he had hoped.

We saw him later than night….. "draggin' main," arm out the window.

Still has that pack of Luckies rolled up in his sleeve.
He was alone.
Diane was at the dance, holding court on the far side of the gym.
She's had so many face lifts that they'll soon be replacing her ears with handles.
I guess she was still attractive, but the cigarette hanging out of the side of her mouth kept drawing my attention.
She was telling her friend how bad her recent x-rays looked, as cigarette ashes dropped on the floor.
I really didn't want that dance with her anymore.
Couple of the geeks from the '60's showed up.
One is a neurosurgeon, another is the CEO of a software company.
Funny, all the ladies want to dance with these guys now.
Wonder why?
And that young lady with the thick glasses and straight hair, who always had her nose buried in a book and was never on the dance floor at those sock hops?
No one noticed her in 1961.
Well, Sandy has written two best-selling novels and owns a publishing company on the east coast.
The woman is stunningly beautiful!
She and her husband had just returned from their winter home in the Caribbean.
Funny, all the guys and gals want to be with her now…..several asked for an autograph.
Wonder why?
The "jock" is still playing the Stones and Beatles, but no one is dancing….afraid they'll pull a hamstring.
Didn't know most of these people, they're old!
How could I be lumped in with this group?
Now I have to admit, that prom night in 1961 still haunts me.
I asked Laurie if she would honor me by stopping by the livestock barn for a dance, it's still there.
She did, and we did.
No formal coat and cumberbund this time, no band, just two old cats in jogging suits, slow dancing under one bare light bulb by the cattle pens.
Oh man, if I could have just ONE THOUSAND more dances with her!
We finished the evening by "dragging main," just the two of us.

I rolled up a bottle of Lipitor in the sleeve of my T-shirt, hung my arm out the window to look cool, then looked over and said: "Would you ever like to return to those days?"

Laurie looked at me with a mischievous smile and said: "When pigs fly."

So…how much of this story is true?

Maybe none…maybe some…maybe all of it.

If you ask me, I'll tell you……when there's pork in the air.

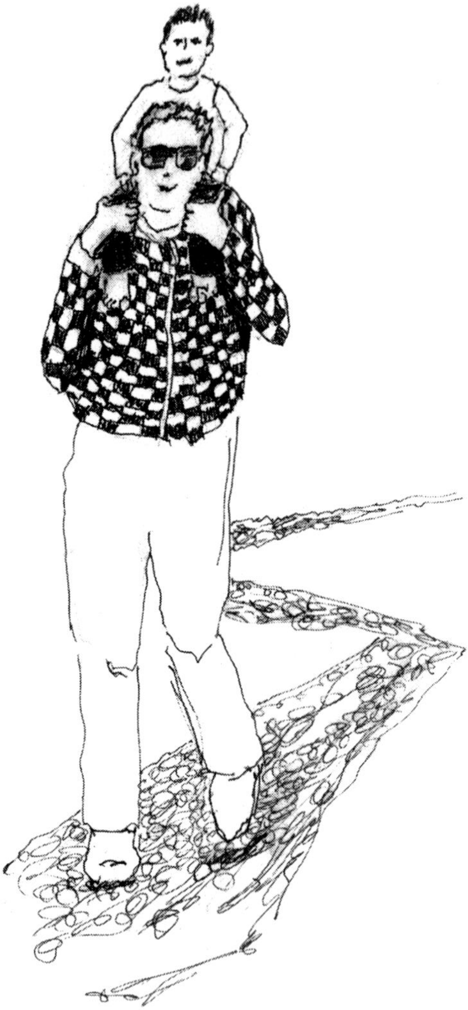

ME AND MY SHADOW

"Grampa, will you take me for a walk?"

The opportunity doesn't present itself nearly enough; so, stuffed with turkey and mashed potatoes on this Thanksgiving afternoon, my grandson and I waddled out the door and down the street.

The curiosity and energy of this three-year-old dynamo has amazed me since he was old enough to scoot around the house.

His motor never stops running.

"Grampa, wait a minute, I see a rock."

That's not all that unusual when you're walking along a gravel road, but the inspection process of a diamond is no more thorough.

The rock went into his pocket.

A myriad of thoughts roam through a grandfather's mind at a time like this, when a small hand is in yours, when bright eyes search for a new prize and tiny feet kick up tiny puffs of dust.

What will he become?

Will he be happy?

Will he have a healthy life?

Is this a future President?

Will he find the cure for cancer?

Will he be a scholar?

Will he be an athlete?

Will he get a job?

My deep thoughts are interrupted.

"Grampa, can you reach that stick?"

As I reached for the dead branch he was pointing to, it dawned on me that he was pointing out my most important task of the day, reaching that stick.

"Thanks grampa."

Don't we all too frequently complicate our lives with things beyond our control, when all we have to do today is "reach that stick?"

My grandson was still bouncing along, poking in the grass with his new stick, and examining more rocks.

By now one pocket was bulging with stones, pulling down his pants.

"Grampa."

"Yeah."

"Will you take me fishing?"

"Today?"

"Yeah!"

"Well, I don't think today, but I will another day."

"Will you be too old then?"

I stopped in my tracks and looked at this little person, who was teaching me lessons in life this Thanksgiving day.

My priorities weren't in order when our daughters were growing up.

There were far too many missed birthdays and plays because of my career.

There wasn't enough time for fishing.

I spent many years making a living, but forgot to make a life.

My grandson is a chance for a do over.

I looked at this little person, who was staring up at me.

"No, I won't be too old."

He bent down to examine another rock, decided it was good enough to keep and stuffed it in his pocket.

He didn't seem to be concerned about my age any longer.

"Grampa."

"Yeah."

"Are you going to die?"

I kneeled down in front of my grandson.

"Why do you ask that?"

"I dunno."

"Yes, I'm going to die."

"When?"

"I don't know."

"Are you afraid?"

"No."

"Why?"

"Because I know where I'm going."

"Can I go with you?"

"I don't think so, not right away, but I'll be waiting for you, so you don't have to be afraid."

"O.K."

By now he had filled his pockets with rocks and his pants were having a very difficult time staying up.

He discovered another prize.

"Do you like this rock Grampa?"

"Yeah."

"Why?"
"I dunno."
"I'm gonna keep it."
"O.K."

I seemed to be adapting myself to his style of conversation.

"Will you carry me?"
"Why?"
"I'm kinda tired."
"O.K."

He was hoisted on my shoulders as we continued our afternoon stroll.

"Do you think I'll ever be big?"
"I think so."
"Why?"
"Because."
"O.K."

He was kicking my ribs like he was riding Sea Biscuit in the home stretch.

"Let's go home," he said.
"Why?"
"Cause my Mom and Dad will want me to come home."
"O.K."
"I guess I can walk now."
"O.K."

The day was growing late.

My grandson looked behind him and said: "Grampa...look!"

He was dancing back and forth, trying to outrun his shadow.

"What is that?"
"It's your shadow."
"What?"
"It's your shadow, it follows you everywhere on a sunny day."
"Why?"
"I dunno."
"O.K."

He danced around a few more times, then stepped in front of me. His shadow disappeared.

"Grampa, where did it go?"
"It became part of my shadow."
"Is that O.K.?"

"Yeah."
"Will it always be a part of your shadow?"
"I hope so."
"Grampa."
"Yeah."
"Am I a part of you?"
"Always."
"Grampa."
"Yeah."
"I love you."
"I love you too."
"Ya want one of my rocks?"
"Can I keep it?"
"Yeah."
"O.K."

We strolled down the lane, my shadow and me, heading home to pumpkin pie and ice cream.

I still have the rock.

It helps me on those days when I forget that all I have to do today is "reach that stick."

GOD'S HERE

"God's here."

It was a statement from my grandson, not an emphatic statement, just a quiet declaration.

"What?"

"God's here," he said again.

"How do you know that?"

"I dunno. I just do."

I looked at this little person, who was content to be searching for bugs in our back yard.

"How long has he been here?" I asked.

"He's always here," came the quiet reply.

Quite a remarkable statement from a four-year-old.

"Can you see him?" I asked.

"Yeah."

"Where?"

"Right here."

He held up a bug for me to examine.

"You think God is a bug?" I asked.

"Yeah."

"Do you talk to God?"

"Yeah."

"What do you say to him?"

"I tell him when I'm afraid."

"Of what?"

"Well Grampa, I'm afraid of a lot of stuff."

"What does he tell you?"

"Not to be afraid."

"Does it help?"

"Yeah."

I turned away so my grandson wouldn't see my tears.

"Grampa?"

"Yeah."

"Are you afraid sometimes?"

"Yeah."

"Do you talk to God even when you're old?"

"All the time."

"What does he say?"
"He tells me not to be afraid."
"Do you feel better then?"
"Yeah."
"Me too," came his reply.
"Grampa?"
"Yeah."
"Do you think God is here now?"
"Yeah."
"Can you see him?"
"Yeah."
"Where?"
"Right here."

I leaned down, picked up my grandson, put him on my shoulders and began walking toward the house.

"Grampa."
"Yeah."
"Your eyes are leaking."
"I know."
"Grampa."
"Yeah."
"I love you."
"I love you too."

Golf Tip:
"Always throw your club forward.
It speeds up the game."

-- Joe Tisserand

A GREAT DAY FOR GOLF?

My buddies, both of them, are starting to talk about golf, that brief period of time up here in the North Country between the 4th of July and Labor Day.

I don't understand why otherwise intelligent people insist on ruining a nice walk by trying to knock that little white ball into a tiny hole some 400 yards away.

I gave up the game years ago.

My golfing ended on a day I was having the best game of my life at a prominent golf resort in south-central Wisconsin.

We lined up on the first tee, which normally was a trauma for me.

Anyone standing on or near the fairway was safe, but anyone in any other position or direction on the golf course within 200 yards of the tee box was fair game.

Believe it or not, I once flailed away, intending to slam a "screamer" some 300 yards down the fairway, and hit a guy BEHIND ME!

Popped that sucker straight up and plunked the guy who was waiting to tee off behind me.

It's tough to come up with a one-liner in these situations.

I blamed the wind.

It was a special day when I was hitting only one off the tee.

Matter of fact, at one time, trying to make a positive out of a negative, I thought about giving lessons on how to relax when you're hitting five off the tee.

In any event, on this day I miraculously hit the ball straight down the middle, dropping it on the lush grass some 250 yards from the tee box.

There was silence on the tee.

Walked up for the second shot, fully intending to rifle one into the woods, but again, miraculously, nailed a three-wood to the green.

I'm "dancin'" in two, putting for the bird.

Oh baby!

As I lined up the putt, I recalled advice a friend had given me on my putting.

"Try to keep it low."

BOOM!

The birdie sings!!!

"Nothin' to this game boys!"

Three shots and already I'm getting cocky.

There is shock registered in the foursome.

Grabbed the ball with a flourish, flipped it in the air, and started off toward Number Two with a swagger.

"Let's tee it up, I believe I have the honors."

Now this was a new experience, after playing golf for 25 years and never getting a chance to take the first shot.

I figure I'm living on borrowed time as I go into the backswing, so "what the hell," I swing from the heels.

BOOM!

Nailed it again, long and high, finally stopped rolling at the 260 mark.

Now the other three are talking among themselves.

I heard Petey say: "He's not that good."

He didn't have to whisper, I agreed with him.

I pull out the 3-wood again, while at the same time trying to calculate the odds of me hitting five good shots in a row.

It didn't look good.

BOOM!

Got ALL of it, sent a three-hopper to within 20 yards of the green on a par five.

Not bad for a guy who has spent more than twenty years perfecting the art of hitting a Nike from the rough after you've hit a Titlist from the tee.

By the way, did I mention that my playing partners were giving me a stroke a hole, two on the par fives?

Now you have to admit, THAT is handicap management.

An EAGLE wouldn't have beaten me on the first hole.

I had to address the situation.

"Boys, an EAGLE isn't even good enough to pluck this duck. Get ready to slap leather."

A smart crack like that probably would have been ok if it hadn't been followed by hysterical laughter….. mine.

The boys were now giving me the stink eye.

Walked up to my ball, looked back at the lads.

"Looks like a soft chipper," I said, followed by a snide grin.

CLICK!

A soft tap from the chipper sends the Nike four feet from the pin.

MORE hysterical laughter….mine.

I've spent a lot of time over the years giving instructions on how to properly line up for your sixth putt, but I DRAINED this one for ANOTHER BIRD on the par five.

More hysterical laughter….this time it wasn't me.

The boys were checking their wallets.

This is fantastic!

Instead of figuring out how to get more distance off a shank, I'm actually playing in the short grass.

Incredible!

Number three…..short Par 3…..slightly uphill…bunker on the left….water in front…180 yards.

Grabbed a five-iron.

"Boys, I believe I still have the honors."

I've been waiting 25 years to say that just ONE time.

I've spent a lot of time over the years figuring out how to avoid the water when you're laying eight in the bunker, so I'm a little skeptical about this hole.

In the back of my mind, as I'm teeing it up, I'm hanging an eyeball on the water and the bunker, thinking: "The birdie is going to fly away and the triple bogy bear is going to eat me up."

Closed my eyes on the backswing this time.

BOOM!

That ball had a crew of five and served dinner….a rainbow arc….dead center.

"Ain't no way it's gonna get there." The Hammer is a skeptic.

"It's wet!" Hopeful thinking from Sully.

THUMP!

ONE HOP….A FOOT FROM THE PIN!

Are you kiddin' me??????

I haven't been that close to the pin on a drive…..EVER!

"Lot of golf left in that shot," Shaky chimes in, but there was no enthusiasm.

Shaky, by the way, skulled his drive, clipped the edge of the bunker and crawled onto the green in three, then chili-dipped a putt.

"I believe you're still out." My response to his misfortunes.

Oh man, ANOTHER thing I haven't had a chance to say in more than two decades of playing this miserable game.

After Shaky takes a six…I step up….DRILL the one-footer and stroll off, without a word, toward Number Four.

Birdie…..THREE in a row!

I notice a lot of mumbling and head shaking behind me.

Inside my head, the "Bluebird of Happiness" is singing a catchy little tune.

Mr. Bluebird is going to gag on that song before the end of the day, but for now, I AM THE MAN!

Step up to Number 4 with adrenaline pumping and body hyperventilating.

Teed 'er up, closed my eyes, swung from the heels.

SWAT!

This one could be trouble, starting to hook toward the rough.

I reach into the bag to grab another ball and hear Sully saying: "Get outta town….I CAN'T believe this!"

I looked up to see the ball bouncing along the asphalt cart path….. CLICK…… CLICK…. CLICK….. CLICK.

Honest to God….it looked like it had a radar lock pulling it along the path.

Five hops along the cart path, caught the edge of the asphalt and jumped ONTO THE GREEN!

I'm on in ONE on a Par 4.

There's nothing more that can be said by anyone in the foursome at this point.

Walk up to the green and take a look at the putt.

About 20 feet, looks like it breaks to the right.

What are the odds?

Pretty good, based on what's happened so far today.

CLICK.

That bad boy is curling toward the cup….could be….might be….it IS!

The EAGLE is in the air!

CA-CHING!!!

Now, I'm on a gravy train with biscuit wheels!

"Boys, they're showin' the replays on ESPN right now. I could set a course record!"

The birdie stopped singin', but it was Par golf on 5….6…7 and 8.

That's right, I'm five…count 'em…five under heading into Nine.

Looks like Nine could be a little dicey.

Par 5…water on the right….woods to the left….bunkers about 280 out and another bunker guarding the front of the green.

Not a problem, I can always play the cart path again.

BOOM!

Duck hooked it into the woods so deep a Puma would be scared trying to find the ball.

Let's see….one in….one out….hitting three.

BOOM!

Skulled it....dribbled it out about 15 yards short of the woman's tee.

This could be embarrassing.

Let's not take chances....let's go to the five iron.

SHA-ZAM!

Hit a rocket into the water.

Let's see...one in the woods...one out....hitting three...skulled one...then one in the water....one out....looks like I'm hitting seven.

Who in hell knows?

I never could figure that out.

Five iron again......skulled it again.....'bout 20 yards past the woman's tee now.

The lads are howling!

Now both my face and other parts of my anatomy are red.

Grabbed another ball.....went to a seven-iron....kept my eye on the ball.

Took a divot the size of a cow pie and watched the ball loop into the water.

WHOOSH.....WHOOSH......WHOOSH.....WHOOSH.....WHOOSH.

Turns out a seven-iron can't swim.

I normally was quite good at finding a ball that everyone else saw go into the water, but the lads were watching me like a hawk, although they we're crying so hard from laughing I doubt they could see me real well.

I hit so many balls into the water that I had to re-grip my ball retriever.

When the pain finally ended, after a four-putt green, I took a 16 on the hole.

Five under going in.....six over coming out.

The lads, wallets intact, headed for lunch while one of the club pro's, who had been watching this debacle, asked me for a moment.

He asked me to tee up a few so he could take a look at my swing.

Teed it up six times....skulled it five times and dribbled it out about ten yards the sixth time.

"What would you suggest?"

It seemed to be a logical question.

He was trying not to laugh when he said: "Another hobby!"

No problem.

He's the professional.

Haven't played since.

PORT WING OPEN

GREATER PORT WING OPEN

The Mayor was kind enough to invite me to participate in the inaugural event of the Greater Port Wing Open this year.

I was honored by the invitation, so I accepted, giving up my lengthy refusal to play the game of golf.

That decision brought me face to face with my golf clubs.

It's been a long time since we visited.

I opened the closet door and immediately was greeted with: "Where have you been for the past six years and why have we been locked in this dark closet?"

The 3-wood apparently had been elected spokesman for the group.

"Do you remember what happened the last time we had you on a golf course? You will pay for this!"

This wasn't starting out well.

I made some weak excuse about a pulled hamstring that hadn't been healing properly, but the clubs didn't buy it.

After all, it has been six years.

The clubs were fighting me as I put them in the dark trunk of the car, despite my assurance they would see the light of day again within the next few hours.

I wasn't feeling enthusiasm, particularly from that 3-wood.

Took nearly three hours to find my golf shoes.

They were wedged under a case of dog food in the back pantry.

Don't understand that....at all.

Damn leather has shrunk over the past six years.

After using two shoehorns to wedge myself into the shoes, the feeling immediately disappeared in all my toes.

My eyes were watering from the pain of the laces digging into my feet but, as a buddy of mine always says: "No pain....no gain."

I've modified that just a bit over the years to, "No pain....no pain," but that doesn't stop the throbbing in my feet.

So, off we go to the GPWO, clumping along in shoes two sizes too small, no feeling in my toes, and hauling renegade clubs.

In the clubhouse, Bucky is putting teams on the board.

If this was a depth chart for a football team, we wouldn't be playing until the next century.

We're the 9th team on the board, starting on the 9th hole and I'm driving cart number 9, wearing size 9 shoes, but we do have five team members, which should give us an advantage, since it's a scramble and everyone gets a shot.

Joyce and Davey are in one cart, Dr. Jim is riding with me and the Colonel is running solo.

I lead off with the 3-wood.

Skulled it, hammered a grass cutter about 20 yards down the fairway.

I swear the 3-wood had a smirk as it went back in the bag.

The Colonel had the best drive, so we circle up for the next shot.

"It's winter rules," says the Colonel.

With that in mind, I tee it up in the fairway for my next shot.

"What are you doing?" the Colonel asks.

"It's winter rules. We'd have to play on top of the snow if it was winter, so I'm reaching for a little elevation here."

The argument didn't fly.

"Drop and give me 20, Porky!" says the Colonel.

Whew, this guy is serious.

I tried, but push-ups at my age just don't work.

I could only do three.

By now, both my feet are numb, right up to the ankle, but the pain is gone.

Let's play golf!

We save face on Number 9 when I snake in a 25-footer for the bird.

We're one under.

I'm thinkin'.... "Dust off that trophy, Daddy's back!"

Daddy left again on Number 1 when I rifled my drive off a tree at the edge of the tee box.

The rebound nearly took out Dr. Jim, who was patiently waiting his turn.

I should mention here that the good doctor still has excellent lateral movement and quickness.

From that point on, I noticed everyone disappeared when I teed up.

Davey seemed to have a reason to bend down and pick something up on the other side of his cart every time I went into my backswing.

Might have been just a coincidence.

Number 4 was a prize hole…..shortest drive for the men.

Taking no chances, I teed it up high and used an eight-iron so I would get some modicum of reasonable distance.

Someone else could have the prize for shortest drive….not me.

Turns out I won four dollars, after popping up the damn ball high enough to file a flight plan and landing it downrange about ten feet.

Davey actually outdid me, strong arming a zinger into the woods off the end of his club, but it didn't reach the fairway.

I'd give Davey two forward yards on the shot, but he was 40 yards deep in the woods, so it didn't count!

I think you now have a pretty good feel of how we're doing after five holes.

By this time, we're thinking Elvis has a better chance of coming back than we do of winning this tournament, so my mind is already wandering as we weave through the woods going to Number 5.

Looking at a stump in the middle of a clearing, I start thinking about the prohibition years, when "stump liquor" was a common practice.

You would go into a clearing, put a dollar on a stump, come back an hour later and there would be some ungodly concoction of alcohol waiting for you in a dirty bottle.

So…back in the "Dirty 30's," two good ol' country boys walk into a clearing and find a "stump bottle."

One of the fellas took out a pistol, held it on his partner and said, "You take a drink otta that bottle."

The frightened man took a gulp and immediately began shaking and gasping for air. As soon as the shaking stops, his partner hands him the pistol and says, "Awright, now you hold the gun on me while I take a snort."

Joyce and Davey are looking at me funny as I start chuckling to myself.

Dr. Jim gives me a nervous smile.

The Colonel has me under surveillance.

I snap back to the tournament in time to watch Dr. Jim drain a 20-footer for par.

We're even for the round, so maybe Elvis hasn't left the building yet.

Then, like a plague, the grasshoppers descended on us.

The Colonel called it survival training.

We fought our way through, but we had a tough go on Number 6.

Survival didn't look good.

The four of us couldn't put together ten yards of distance if we added up all our shots on the drive, so it was up to the Colonel to save us.

He scooted his drive into the rough, then caught one off the toe of a 4-wood for his second shot, lobbing a round into the jungle at a 90-degree angle.

The Colonel wasn't happy.

We planned to drop and give him a courtesy 20, but I was afraid I couldn't get back up again, Davey was picking something up on the other side of his cart, Joyce had ducked behind her bag and Dr. Jim was heading for the beverage cart.

Now.....Elvis is in the limo.

We're two over and out of it.

Davey had a personal best on Number 7 when he did a four-tree bank shot with his drive and still landed in fair territory.

Both he and Dr. Jim got into a little trouble on this hole when they were caught talking in the middle of the Colonel's backswing, just before he drilled one into the pond.

Without direction, they both dropped and gave him five, which I thought was an excellent effort at that particular point in the round.

We headed back to the clubhouse to bask in the afterglow and total up the damage.

I lost 13 balls in 9 holes on a wide-open golf course.

That could be a personal best.

My play had deteriorated even further from the last time I played the game, six years ago.

As I put the clubs into the trunk, the 3-wood couldn't resist one final shot, "Any questions?"

Smart ass.

None of our group made the All-Tournament team.

Three under won it. Four over was the high gross.

I walked over and sat down beside the Colonel.

"Jeet yet?" I asked.

"No...ju?" he questioned back.

"Nah, but I'm ready for a sandwich."

The Colonel and me saddled up and headed home for supper.

We can't wait for next year's GPWO.

THE OLD MAN AND ME

THE OLD MAN AND ME

The white haired man sits across from his son.

He's old, very ill, and they both know this will be the last chance they have to visit.

The distance between them is great, the time is short.

They both know he is dying.

The white haired man struggles for every breath, fogging the mask that brings oxygen to his battered lungs, scarred by 30 years of smoking three packs of cigarettes a day.

The white mane falls back on the couch as he struggles for his next breath.

His son feels helpless.

"You know, dad, there are a lot of things we should talk about."

The old man looked at his son.

"And what would they be?" he quietly gasps.

"Well," the son begins, "I caused you a lot of grief when I was young. I remember one time you came to watch me at baseball practice. I told you to go home, I didn't want you there.

I know that hurt you.

You made it seem like it wasn't a big deal, but I saw you hang your head when you walked out of the park. I've felt bad about that day for over 40 years, but I was never man enough to apologize to you for being a fool and treating my father with such inexcusable disrespect.

I feel terrible about that incident to this day.

I'm sorry."

"You were young," he said softly.

"That's no excuse," the son replied.

"Dad, you've done a lot of sensitive and caring things for me over the years.

You never forgot my birthday.

I always knew I'd get another newly minted silver dollar on my birthday.

I cherish them.

You always had to ask me if I got the package.

I never called to say: "thank you."

I'm sorry, I should have been more sensitive."

"Ah, I know you liked them," comes the gentle response. "It's not a big deal."

"Yes, it is a big deal!" says the son. "I wish I could go back and do a lot of things over in my relationship with you."

Tears welled up in the son's eyes.

He took a deep breath, then continued.

"Dad, I know you waited every Father's Day for my card.

I missed way too many by not taking the time to send one to you.

I always had good intentions, but it seemed that something always came up that delayed the card until it was too late.

That's no excuse.

I'm sorry."

"I did enjoy the cards you sent," he says.

"I didn't send enough," says the son, his eyes on the floor.

"I missed a lot of opportunities to say things I've wanted to over the years, to make things right between us," whispers the son.

"Well, you're making them right now," the father replies.

"Have you made your peace with God?" the son questions.

"I have," comes the reply through the oxygen mask.

"Are you afraid?"

"No," the father answers.

"That gives me some comfort," the son replies.

"Dad, there's something I want to say to you that I never have.

I don't know why.

It's always been there, in my heart, but you've never heard it from me."

"What's that?" he says.

"I love you, Dad."

"I know. I love you too."

The son looks at his father, once a strong, 260-pound man's man, now reduced to less than 100 pounds.

He leans over and hugs the frail man.

That's the way I pictured the final conversation with my father would end.

We both knew he was dying, that time was short.

Nonetheless, the final conversation never happened.

I always had good intentions.

I even rehearsed what I would say in our final visit to make things right in our relationship.

I was never sure if those rehearsals were for him or to ease the guilt that I've carried with me for all these years.

Now, as I write this story, kneeling before a white cross that marks his grave at a military cemetery, there's no more time.

It has expired, as has he.

I wish there was one more chance for us to have that final conversation, man to man.

We still have a lot of things to talk about.

The most difficult burden I still carry is that I never told my father that I loved him.

It was always there, in my heart, but it never came out.

It still hasn't, but as I spend time alone with him on this summer afternoon, under a bright, blue, sky, with the manicured grass still wet from a morning shower and birds singing in the trees, I hope my heart can send the message in death that I didn't send in life.

I hope his soul can hear me on this beautiful afternoon.

"I love you dad."

AN EMOTIONAL DAY

Every now and again, something catches me by surprise and leaves me totally speechless.

A few months back, a story appeared in this column entitled: "The Old Man and Me."

As sometimes happens, a story will touch the lives, or the hearts, of a number of readers and generate comments to me or someone associated with the paper.

I'm always pleased to hear that one of my stories has touched someone's heart.

This particular story is a case in point.

I didn't keep track of the number of people who commented on "The Old Man and Me," but it was a goodly number.....a large number, actually, for a small newspaper.

The story was written, in its entirety, while I was kneeling in front of a white military grave marker at Fort Snelling National Cemetery in St. Paul, Minnesota.

The name on the marker is: Odean M Perkins....PFC...U.S. Army.

Odean was a veteran of World War Two.

He was engaged in heavy fighting on the island of Leyte, in the Philippines.

Like many men of his generation, he was an American hero who saved our way of life.

Odean was my father.

I'm not ashamed to say I was crying when I wrote the story.

I am ashamed to say that I never said "I love you" to my dad, even though the words were always in my heart.

The story outlined the regrets I had in my father's final days, my regret that I never said "I love you" and my regret that I didn't treat him with the respect he deserved when I was growing up.

It was a difficult story to write.

I had been thinking about it for five years, since the day he died, but I could never find the words.

When I kneeled at his grave, the words were there.

The story was written in ten minutes on the back page of a magazine.

I never changed a word from the original draft.

Most of us are hesitant to share our deepest feelings with others.

We are hesitant to expose our emotions and shortcomings, but sometimes the feelings are so deep that the sharing becomes a catharsis.

That frequently is the case with me.

Some of the stories I write are silly, some are sad, some touch on an incident that has inspired me, and still others tear at my emotions.

A friend stopped by our house after the story was published and asked if I was talking about my father.

Several folks said it made them cry and then there was the man in Poplar.

I was leaving the Poplar grocery store when I heard a voice behind me say, "Are you Gary Perkins?"

I turned to see a middle-aged man.

"Yes, I am," I replied. "What can I do for you?"

The man looked at me for a long moment, then said, "I got a copy of that article you wrote on the old man.

I just wanted you to know that I hadn't talked to my dad in 15 years. I called him last week. Just wanted you to know."

I knew I should reply. I wanted to, but I couldn't get the words out.

He must have wondered what kind of a rude mute he was talking to as I stood there with my mouth open and tears running down my cheeks.

"Well, just wanted you to know," he repeated.

As he got in his car, I managed to croak, "Thank you," but he was already gone.

I have no idea who this man is, I have no idea how he knew me.

It never occurred to me to ask his name.

To you, sir, my deepest apologies for my behavior.

I just want you to know that you deeply touched my heart with those few words.

If I had managed to compose myself, I would have asked you one question.

When you made that call to your dad, did you say: "I love you?"

If you didn't……please call again.

MICE

MICE!

I must confess that writers, at least this one, tend to expand journalistic license beyond the limits of believability, from time to time, over some of the most ordinary things that happen in everyday life, leaving fact and fiction totally confused.

Fact of the matter is, we have mice in our house.

Well, a mouse...actually.

That's not an altogether pleasant thought, but it's not the end of the world either, unless you're speaking to my wife.

It seems the little creatures want to join us every fall, just about the time the weather turns to chilly nights with a hint of frost.

I would suppose the mice, like us humans, begin looking for somewhere warm to spend the cold days and nights ahead.

Laurie does not want our house to become their winter condominium.

Consequently, witness, if you will, a pleasant fall evening in the great room of a home in northern Wisconsin, near the shore of Lake Superior.

Grampa Perkins reaches down to grab a book.

Movement along the wall is felt out of the corner of his eye.

"I'll be damned," he says. "We have a mouse."

There is no hesitation in Laurie's scream.

"Aaaaaaaaaaaaaaaaaaaahhhhhhhhhhhhhhhhhhhhh!"

I didn't know that a 56-year-old woman, with bad knees, could jump straight up from a chair, clearing the cushion by a good twelve inches, and land with her feet under her behind.

The little creature creeping along the wall even stopped and stared.

I thought he was going to begin applauding with his little feet.

Instead, he nonchalantly continued his trip along the wall, then disappeared under one of our end tables.

"Oh my god!" Laurie pants. "We've got to get him!"

That's difficult to do when you are plastered against the back of a recliner, with your hands on your head and your toes beating a tattoo on the leather.

"We" means "me."

I, personally, have nothing against mice.

They're cute little creatures, but I suppose they could pose a problem if left unchecked, so I begin putting together a plan to take out the little bugger.

It's a mouse.

How tough could it be?

The plan begins with a direct frontal attack to drive him out of his sanctuary under the end table, then eliminate the threat with a rolled up newspaper.

For the next ten minutes I initiate a "shock and awe" assault on his command and control center, our end table.

I'm on my knees, pounding on the end table with one hand in a constant barrage, while my other hand, raised high in the air, holds the heavy artillery, a rolled up newspaper.

For the first few minutes I actually felt sorry for the little guy, but then my hand started to hurt from the constant pounding and my arm was quivering from holding the newspaper in the air.

No mouse.

My knees started to throb from the massive weight they were supporting.

Laurie has not moved.

After ten minutes, I'm starting to think this mouse is a little tougher than I initially thought.

Apparently he was dug in pretty good in his end table bunker.

I leaned down to get a better look.

Bam!!

That damn mouse came streaking out from under the end table, ran smack into my glasses, bounced off, and went flying along the wall into the kitchen.

Mice look a lot bigger when you're at their level and they run directly into your eye.

I jumped up, slammed my head against the coffee table, nearly knocking myself cold, stumbled against a chair, and wound up flat on my back in the middle of the room.

"You o.k.?"

Always good to hear concern from my wife, but I noticed she hadn't moved one inch since the battle began.

"Course I am," comes the quick reply.

How could you admit a mouse just scared the hell out of you?

"It's just going to take a little longer than I thought."

Vicious creatures, these mice.

I limped into the kitchen, trying to formulate a new battle plan through the throbbing pain in my head.

The right side of my glasses was smudged where the mouse had slammed into the lens.

I thoughtfully wiped off my glasses as I scoped out the kitchen, looking for the probable bunker that was hiding the creature.

Could be we're going to have to run a trap line...might go with the peanut butter "snapper," with a "sticky" trap back-up.

Slap those babies along the wall with chunky peanut butter....problem solved!

No mouse at the end of the first day, but the peanut butter is gone from two of the traps.

"Did I put peanut butter on those traps?"

At my age, you're never quite certain if you did what you thought you did in the manner that you thought you did it.

So, out comes the chunky peanut butter.

I get the traps re-baited, reach back for the peanut butter jar and set my hand on one of the "sticky" traps.

As I jump up to shake this thing off my hand, I step onto one of the peanut butter traps.

Snap!

"Yeeeeeeeeeeeeeeeeeeeeeeeeeooooooooooooooowwwwwwwwww w!!!"

Now I've got a mousetrap snapped on my little toe, a sticky trap on one hand, and a nasty vocabulary.

I'm dancing through the kitchen when Laurie looks down from the upstairs balcony and says: "Will you quit fooling around down there and get that mouse?"

I'm about to reply when, out of the corner of my eye, I see the target streaking along the wall, nose down, tail up, all four legs at warp speed, flat out for the end table.

The nasty vocabulary intensifies.

I leap at the beast, with a "sticky" trap on one hand and a peanut butter trap flapping off my little toe.

I swipe at the creature and miss, slapping the "sticky" trap on the wall.

"Oh boy, that's gonna leave a mark," Laurie comments from the balcony.

I thank Laurie in the appropriate manner for her observation as I try to pull the "sticky" trap off the wall and my hand.

My mind is foggy from the pain generated by the trap still flapping on the end of my little toe.

As I gingerly reach down to remove the trap, the mouse casually saunters out from under the end table and begins to nibble on the peanut butter in still another trap.

It doesn't snap!

Are you kiddin' me?

I've got a trap hanging off the end of my little toe, while the mouse is having a stress free lunch.

I dive at the target.

Zoom!

He's back in command and control under the end table.

Snap!

"Aaaaaaaaaaaaaaaaaaaaaaaaaaaaaaaahhhhhhhhhh!"

Now I've got a peanut butter trap snapped on my right hand, a "sticky" trap on my left hand and another peanut butter trap cutting off the circulation in my little toe.

The vocabulary has now deteriorated to the lowest common denominator.

"I've never heard some of those words," says wife Laurie. "Quit playing with those traps, we have to catch that mouse."

Battle lines are now drawn.

We need a mouser!

With that thought in mind, I step out the back door and start looking for one of the neighborhood cats.

There's always two or three patrolling the perimeter.

Now, how do I recruit one of these lads to the battle?

A tasty container of 2% milk and a piece of leftover bacon should be the combination that does the trick...both are placed on the rear deck.

Half an hour later, I have volunteers, a herd of them.

There must be 15 cats lapping up milk and fighting over the bacon.

It sounded like the Texas chain saw massacre.

The wailing and gnashing of teeth was something to behold as I reached down to grab the milk dish.

Four cats pounce on me, while two others sink their nails into my leg.

I just wanted one mouser!

I have deranged monsters!

Thinking quickly, I grabbed one of the more docile cats and brought him, I think it was a him, who knows, into the house.

This was another mistake in my strategic planning.

Rocky and Rose, our two dogs, have heard the commotion and are waiting for us when we open the door.

Immediately, I was in the middle of a firefight.

Rock and Rose were barking hysterically, climbing my legs, trying to get at the cat, while the cat began hissing, flipped out the claws, jumped over my head onto my back, where he, or she, took up a defensive position, after digging his, or her, claws deep into my back.

Now we have the dogs barking, the cat hissing, and me screaming like a banshee while I'm running through the house, trying to get the cat off my back.

Rocky gets between my scrambling feet, causing me to trip and fall in a heap, face down in front of the couch.

The cat takes off at a dead run up the stairs, with Rock and Rose in pursuit, one of them hissing, two barking.

I look up and see the mouse quietly nibbling on the peanut butter in a trap along the wall.

To add insult to injury, Laurie picks up the terrified cat and says, "What did you do to this poor creature?"

The dogs are sitting on their behinds, tails wagging, gazing up adoringly at Laurie and the cat.

I have no intelligent response to Laurie's question.

The mouse saunters back under the end table.

Lunch is over.

No more mister nice guy.

I pick up the end table, his command and control center, to smoke him out.

He streaks along the wall when he's flushed, jumps over...that's right.... jumps over... the peanut butter trap, detours around the sticky trap, busts a move on me when I swipe at him with a rolled up newspaper, and disappears under the refrigerator.

Laurie, the cat, and two dogs are watching this great performance from the balcony.

They look like they are going to burst out in spontaneous applause.

This mouse is tougher than nails.

Quite frankly, I'm starting to develop an appreciation for the little bugger myself.

Laurie brings the cat, which is now purring contently in her arms, downstairs, fills a saucer with milk and sets him, or her, down.

Rock and Rose watch quietly while our mouser drinks the milk.

I see the mouse peeking out from under the refrigerator.

The battle is not going well.

I decide to attempt negotiation.

"Ya know," I say to my beautiful wife, "It's a little mouse, what can he hurt?"

He can hurt me, but I say that to myself.

"He does have a big heart," comes the reply from Laurie.

Rock and Rose nod their heads....the cat doesn't care. He, or she, is still head down in the milk.

"All right then," comes my confident reply. "Let's take a new tack. Let's ignore the little bugger and see what happens. Matter of fact, let's welcome him into the family."

I get tentative agreement for a short term truce.

To make it even more interesting, I take a small butter dish, label it "Mick the Magnificent," spoon on a generous dab of peanut butter and set it beside the dogs water dish.

This mouse is a player.

He recognizes quickly that we are no match for his abilities.

I think we bored him.

His dish is still there, with the peanut butter, but we haven't seen Mick since that day.

Problem solved.

A mouse in your house?

How tough can it be?

Ya just gotta be smarter than the mouse.

At this point, you have to wonder when the writer lost control of truth versus fiction.

That mouse knows!

Washin' Trucks at the Fire Hall

WASHIN' TRUCKS AT THE FIRE HALL

We had a truck washing night at the Port Wing fire hall last week.

Truth be told, I would just as soon kiss a wolverine as wash and polish fire trucks.

Normally, I whine and moan enough to get out of it, or I find a reasonable excuse not to show up, but the Chief busted a move on me that caught me by surprise, got me to make a commitment to show up.

Whaddya gonna do?

I said I'd be there, so off I go, lower lip puffed out, kickin' stones all the way.

As soon as I arrive, I notice everyone is wearing turnout boots to keep their feet dry.

TA-DAH!

Here's my out.

"Ah Chief, I haven't got turnout boots that fit me. Don't want to go wading through the water with these skimpy shoes."

Before the Chief can respond, Jerry comes cruisin' by with drying rags draped over both arms.

"Hey," he says, "Good news, your boots are here. They're in the back room."

Damn!

Looks like I'm involved.

There are five firefighters crawling all over the Number One pumper, with Jeff serving as the hose man.

I begin plotting to get the hose from Jeff, but he's too crafty for me.

He looks at me with a smile: "Got a lot of rags there, Gary."

Caught.........like a rat in a trap.

It's tough to plot when a person is smiling at you.

I volunteered to take the trucks for an "air drying" run on I-13.

I told the Chief I could test the lights and siren at the same time.

That didn't fly.

Finally, tired of my whining, the Chief assigned me to "buffing and polishing," which put me inside the fire hall, where I couldn't affect attitudes.

Little did I know that Jimmy "Buff-It" would be in charge of the detail.

This guy comes in with equipment that could start a commercial car wash.

I quietly started slinking toward the rear door.

"Hey, where ya goin'?"

I could see no reasonable means of escape.

"Why don't you grab that can of wax and start shining up the chrome?"

Caught again…like a bear with his paw in a honey pot.

"Let's git 'er done!"

Jimmy "Buff-It" is chortling as he pulls out extension cords, buffing pads, cans of wax, and various buffing machinery that requires electricity.

I'm hoping for an alarm….no luck.

Grabbing a rag, I sullenly begin applying wax to the chrome on the Number One pumper.

For those of you who aren't firefighters, do you have ANY idea how much chrome there is on a fire truck?

It is endless!

Who's in charge of building these things anyway?

This isn't a car show!

Jimmy "Buff-It" is singing some song about margarita's as I mumble to myself.

He's got some kind of electric buffing machinery working wax into the front fender.

I look up to make a smart comment and……...ZING!

The buffing pad flys off the electric buffer and shoots by my head like a bat after a mosquito.

Jimmy "Buff-It" gives me the slippery grin.

"Guess I had 'er on a little loose."

I look at the Chief and say: "That could have knocked me silly!"

"I know," the Chief replies with a smile.

I'm thinking to myself that this trauma should excuse me for the rest of the night when Jimmy "Buff-It" says, "Ya wanna grab that pad? We gotta get goin'!"

Where's the empathy for my near miss?

I decided my dignity had been insulted, so I went home.

"How come you're home so early?" The question comes from my smiling wife.

Again….the smile.

"They were teasing me," I said, "so I came home!"

She made me go back to the fire hall.

I walk in to find Jimmy "Buff-It" elbow deep in wax, happily whistling to himself as he checks his teeth in the shine on a fender.

I'm back to rubbin' chrome, grumbling to myself.

Jimmy "Buff-It" keeps throwing rags on the hood of Number One, but they keep sliding off.

No wonder, gotta be three inches of wax up there.

Jimmy puts his foot on the gleaming metal step of the pumper and grabs the door handle to pull himself up into the cab.

His foot slips off the overwaxed step and the resulting fall rips his hand off the handle.

The "J" man goes down hard, rattling his chin off the step, but he's back up like a fighter with an eight-count....head flying in all directions.

"No problem....I'm good...I'm OK."

We know he's loopy when he tells me, for no apparent reason, to "throw a little extra wax on the steering wheel."

Now there's a good idea.

Let's wax up that steering wheel so we look like an octopus in a school of mackerel when we try to turn a multi-ton vehicle, with 1500-gallons of water in the tank serving as a booster rocket.

I jump in to take charge of the situation.

"You're hurt champ, let's go back to your corner and get ready for the next round."

"We've got a mouse in the house." A low rumble comes from Jimmy "Buff-It."

"Sure we do champ, let's get you set down over here."

"Gotta get that mouse, he's right over there."

The "J" man points toward the back of the truck, but his eyes are rolling like the reels on a slot machine, so I don't pay much attention.

"No problem champ, we'll get that mouse."

"Damn mice can chew a hole in the drop tanks." The "J" man mumbles.

Now, admittedly, that would be a problem.

If we have a hole in the drop tanks, we have a situation in the event of an incident requiring a large amount of water beyond the capacity of the pumper.

In such an incident, the tanker trucks fill the drop tank, then shuttle back for another load, while the pumper is using the water dumped in the drop tank.

The process continues until the incident is cleared.

That's why the drop tanks are routinely inspected.

I feel bad for Jimmy.

He took a dirty hit, now he's hallucinating about mice in the firehouse.

"That's great....that's just great!" Dale is grumbling in the back of the hall.

"What's up?" asks the Chief.

Dale has one of the drop tanks on the floor.

"Looks like a mouse chewed a hole in the canvas," comes the reply.

The drop tank is pulled out of service as the search begins for the gnarly gnawer.

Turns out Jimmy "Buff-It," in his altered state, DID see a mouse.

"We gotta find that mouse, or we've got a continuing problem," says the Chief.

The officers of the PWFD huddle together to determine what action needs to be taken to track down the offending critter.

There was talk of forming a committee, mousers, negotiation and direct frontal attacks with snapper traps.

It was beginning to look like it would take a little time to form a consensus.

I looked over to see how Jimmy "Buff-It" was doing.

He's leaned over in the chair, with his tongue hanging out, eyes still bouncing around like a kid on a pogo stick.

"Got the mouse," he mumbles with a slack jawed smile.

"What?"

"Got the mouse," he repeats.

I look at the "J" man's large fist to see the head and front paws of a mouse peeking out.

"Jimmy, don't squeeze the mouse," I plead.

"Nah," he says, "We're friends. He just came up to me and jumped in my hand. Says he knows you. His name is Mick."

Sweet Jesus!!!!!

It was Mick the Magnificent, the mouse that was using our home as a condo a few months ago.

"I invited Mick out ta home, want him to meet Ceil," the "J" man says with a goofy grin. "Might invite him to move in."

He takes Mick by the tail and drops him in his shirt pocket, then looks at me again with that goofy grin while one eye rolls back in his head.

Mick pops up his head and gives me a wink.

We leave the officers discussing strategy and head for Jimmy "Buff-It's" house.

I want to be there when Ceil meets Mick.

HOWARD'S CHICKENS

HOWARD AND HIS CHICKENS

My friend Howard, over in Herbster, has lost his chickens.

Biddy One went first....too many times in the food dish ...Goshawk got the other two.

Damndest thing I've ever seen...those chickens.

If you don't know Howard, he has Santa's workshop in the back room of the Northern Lights gift shop.

He's a master craftsman, and a good share of the South Shore has at least one piece of furniture that Howard has lovingly created, but woodworking is only one of Howard's unique talents.

Howard talks to critters...and they talk back.

The first time I met Howard, I showed up in his workshop to find him leaning down on one knee, talking to a chicken.

Her name was Biddy.

Howard would say something...Biddy would look up at him and cluck a few times.

Seemed like they understood each other.

Howard apparently didn't think any of this was unusual, since he didn't even mention the chicken when we started talking about cabinets.

We would move to the other side of the workshop, Biddy would trail along behind Howard, just like a puppy.

After about 15 minutes, Biddy stepped between us and started clucking like a fox had just stepped into the henhouse.

Howard looked down at her and said: "She thinks you're taking up too much of my time. We'll have to carry on with this later."

I'm thinking: "I've been thrown out of better joints than this....but never by a chicken."

Howard ambled over toward the corner, grabbed a handful of chicken feed, went back down on one knee, and started talking to the chicken again.

Biddy would quietly cluck an answer to Howard while she dined.

I thought it best to leave the two of them alone.

Wasn't too much later that Biddy One turned in her feathers.

She weighed 16 pounds and looked like a water bed sloshing from side to side when she walked, so I guess it was the ten meals a day that made her go toes up.

I felt bad for Howard.

The next time I went to Santa's workshop, I was greeted by two chickens.

Howard felt if there are two, they will have each other to visit with when he's not in the shop.

He named them Biddy Two and Henny.

Biddy Two was the smaller of the two…... she was a tattler.

Every now and again, Biddy Two and Henny would sneak over to the neighbor's yard.

Howard didn't like that, so he would go over to the neighbors and herd them back to the shop, giving them a stern lecture along the way.

They're CHICKENS……how could they understand a stern lecture?

A few weeks after I watched Howard herd the dynamic duo back home from the neighbors, we're visiting in the back room of his shop.

Here comes Biddy Two, clucking up a storm as she trots in the door.

Biddy Two charges right up to Howard and starts pecking at his trousers to get his attention.

Howard shoos her away.

"Get otta here Biddy, we're talking."

Biddy Two starts pecking at his shoe, takes a few steps toward the door, comes back and starts pecking at his shoe again.

"What do you want?" asks Howard.

Biddy Two takes two steps toward the door, looks at Howard, takes two steps toward him, then heads for the door again.

"OK," Howard says. "Show me."

Biddy Two leads Howard into the neighbor's yard, where we find Henny busily scratching up grubs in the lawn.

Now Biddy Two gives Henny the stern lecture, while Henny is loudly clucking back at her, obviously saying: "Leave me alone, you're scaring the grubs"…….until Henny sees Howard.

She gives it the "Oh boy, the old man is here" look, then trots back to the woodshop with Biddy Two trotting behind her, clucking all the way.

I looked at Howard and said: "I can't believe this!"

Howard had a simple answer.

"Critters can tell when you like them and understand them, so can kids. You can't fool 'em."

I noticed he didn't say anything about adults.

A short time after that, Howard returned to his workshop after lunch one afternoon and found both Biddy Two and Henny in their outside pen.

They had been attacked and killed.

Howard laid them both to rest.

Later that day, he and his wife, Sally, were spending a few moments outside the shop by the pen of Biddy Two and Henny.

They looked up and saw a Goshawk perched in a tree, staring down at them.

As Howard tells it: "He would look at me, then look at the pen, then back at me, like he was saying, what did you do with my chickens?"

Howard assumes he found the critter that attacked Biddy Two and Henny, but not surprisingly, Howard has no animosity toward the Goshawk.

He said: "Ya know, I felt better after that. The hawk was just doing what he had to do to stay alive."

There have been no more chickens in the workshop since Biddy One, Biddy Two and Henny.

I have never asked Howard why, but as I look down at our two dogs, Rocky and Rosie, I think I know.

It's just too damn painful when they leave.

Incidentally, Howard was over to the house a few days ago.

Rocky jumped onto his lap as soon as he sat down and stayed there, contentedly wagging his tail and licking Howard's hand.

Rocky NEVER does that for ANYONE….including ME.

I love that dog.

I even stoop to bribing him with treats to get him to jump up on my lap in the evening.

Rock always grabs the treat, but no lap time for me.

Howard quietly talks to Rock, while patting his back.

Rock is talking back, making little growling sounds when Howard asks a question.

Incredible!

What can you say about this gentle man who talks to chickens and other critters?

The only thing I can think of is: "Good on ya, Howard, good on ya."

Howard has a gift.

I wish I had it!

Don't you?

"Think of three things . . .
whence you came,
where you are going,
and to whom you
must account."

-- Benjamin Franklin

THE LADIES OF THE SOUTH SHORE

We are lucky enough to have a good many distinguished citizens living along the South Shore of Lake Superior. Some have lived in this area since the early 1900's, and they have wonderful stories of their formative years.

When these octogenarians were in their youth, times were different, a lot different than they are today.

Early in their childhood years, radio was still in its infancy, and no one had heard of anything like television or video games.

As children, they made their own fun. Family life was held in high regard.

Simple joys were cherished each day.

If I may, I'd like to take a few minutes to introduce you to two of these distinguished ladies….. Holly Carlson of Port Wing, and Gert Diamon, originally from the village of Herbster.

I think you will agree, both have lived through remarkable times.

Please join me now, as we reflect back to how it was in 1928, just a short time before the stock market crash in 1929 that signaled the start of the Great Depression in America.

SWENSON'S WIGWAM HOTEL

A lot of cool things happened in 1928.

Penicillin, Vitamin C, and bubble gum all came to life.

Amelia Earhart became the first woman to fly across the Atlantic in 24 hours and 49 minutes.

It took the Yankees just four games to sweep the Cardinals in the World Series.

The "Babe" had three home runs in the fourth game, but Lou Gehrig was the star of the series with a .525 batting average, four home runs, and 9 RBI's.

Disney studios began working on the first Mickey Mouse cartoon and Robert Swenson brought his family from Scandia, Minnesota to Port Wing, Wisconsin.

The arrival of the Swenson family in Port Wing, while perhaps not of the same magnitude as the other events, nonetheless marked the beginning of a family hotel business that lasted more then a quarter century.

The original plan of the Swenson family was to set up a farming operation on 80 acres of land they had purchased in Orienta Township, but that plan never materialized.

It seems the Wigwam Hotel was up for sale when they arrived.

An offer was made to, and accepted, by the Okerstrom family, owners of the Wigwam, and the Swenson family quickly transformed from farmers to innkeepers.

In the blink of an eye, Robert Swenson began a new adventure with his wife, Maria, his four daughters, Ruby, Marvel, Laverne and the youngest, Holly, who was five years old at the time, two dogs, and a cat.

The two oldest daughters, Elaine and Hazel, had already left the nest, gotten married, and started their own families.

The hotel was vacant at the time it was purchased by the Swenson family, so the first order of business was to get the place in shape to welcome guests.

Let's keep in mind that, at this point in Port Wing history, Main Street, which is now Washington Avenue, the road leading down to the marina, was nothing more than a rutted wagon track.

Sidewalks were made of wood, there was no indoor plumbing.

Holly tells us there was running water, as long as their legs held up.

The Swenson girls had to run to the neighbors to get it, and then bring the water back in buckets.

Later on there was a cistern at the hotel and a hand pump in the kitchen, but it didn't start out that way.

There were challenges to be faced and conquered for 26 years, until the family got out of the business in 1954, leaving behind a treasure chest of memories.

The Wigwam Hotel still stands today.

It is located on the East side of Washington Avenue, one building down from Gary Sherman's law office.

The Wigwam is now a private home, owned by Nora Tribys.

Back in 1928, the Wigwam was surrounded by a bustling Port Wing business district, energized by dairy farming and private business operations.

There were also a number of large strawberry fields in the area.

Logging was on the decline by the late 1920's.

Next to the Wigwam was the office of Bayfield Electric.

That building is still standing today.

There were three grocery stores located on Washington Avenue.

Ogren's store was located where Milt and Esther Ollenberger now live.

Albert Peterson had a grocery store north of Ogren's store, and Bagstad's was located on the corner of Washington Avenue and School Road.

If you drive by the former Bagstad's location today, you will see the block building still standing at the rear of the lot.

Bread sold for 9 cents a loaf, and a dozen eggs could be purchased for 20 cents a dozen.

If you were willing to take cracked eggs, you could shave a few cents off the cost.

Directly across the street from Bagstad's was Buchholz Hardware.

That location is now an empty lot.

The post office was north of the Lundgren Block.

The Globe Tavern was located in the Lundgren Block in the late 30's and early 40's.

Al Lundgren, the owner, had a loudspeaker installed outside the tavern on dance nights, when the CCC (Civilian Conservation Corps) guys would come to town.

The CCC guys would arrive in the back of a truck, singing at the top of their lungs.

When they left for the night, the loudspeaker was still blaring, encouraging them to sing even louder on the way home, no doubt fortified by several adult beverages.

The Port Wing Creamery was located where the town garage is now.

The Creamery was widely known throughout the area for its excellent butter product.

When Holly Swenson was a young girl, she and her friends would stop by the Creamery and Paul Hogfeldt would give them a chunk of freshly churned butter.

The Port Wing Co-Op was located south of the Creamery in later years.

Andy Gidlof sold gas and repaired cars in his shop on Washington Avenue.

There were also five churches in Port Wing back in 1928.

Today there is one church.

The daughters of Robert Swenson worked hard at the hotel, seven days a week, but it was a fun time and there were certain things you looked forward to at the end of the week.

On special occasions, after the work was done at the hotel, the Swenson girls were allowed to trot across the street to the Lundgren Block for an ice cream cone.

The cost...5 cents.

If they were lucky, Dad would also spring for a bottle of pop, which would set him back another 5 cents.

Total cost to buy the four Swenson girls an ice cream cone and a bottle of pop...40 cents.

The Wigwam Hotel had five guestrooms and a large dining room.

There was a large porch attached to the front of the building, a large gathering room next to the dining room and an office to conduct business.

The third floor was one large room, with a view of Lake Superior.

The Swenson girls called that floor "the tower."

There were also two bedrooms that were used as family quarters.

Space was at a premium in the family area, which meant the girls had to sleep three to a bed.

It was COLD in the winter.

Like most buildings of that era, there was, at best, a small amount of insulation in the walls, and that was frequently old newspaper.

It was COLD!

The hotel was heated entirely by wood during the winter months.

Maria and girls were up early every day, normally 4:30 or 5:00, preparing breakfast for the guests and getting the hotel ready for the day.

Breakfast was served promptly at 6:00 a.m.

Wood had to be brought in for the cook stove, water from the well, ice from the icehouse.

The cook stoves had to be fired up, coffee made, eggs and salt pork fried, milk poured, bread toasted in large wire racks over the wood cook stove and then drenched with pure country butter.

The guests, literally, ate it up.

One guest insisted on getting up early and joining the girls in the kitchen, so he could see how that "wonderful" toast was made every morning.

However, the Swenson girls didn't eat the same breakfast.

After the guests had been served, the tables cleaned and the dishes washed, the girls would have a bowl of cereal, then trot off to school.

By the way, with no sewer or running water, Maria and the Swenson girls were also sanitation engineers.

That means they were in charge of changing and cleaning the chamber pots in the guestrooms, right after breakfast, each day.

Whew!!!!

After school, Maria and the girls were back on the job again, getting ready for the evening meal which, like all meals at the Wigwam, was served family style.

The evening meal was served promptly at 6:00 p.m.

Here's a menu for a typical evening meal at the Wigwam back in the late 20's and early 30's:

>
> 1931
> WIGWAM HOTEL
> EVENING MENU
> ------------------------
>
> Meatballs
> Mashed potatoes
> Homemade bread
> Pure, 100%, country butter
> Beans or carrots
> Homemade pie
> Coffee and milk

The cost?

A room plus three meals a day…. $25 a month.

If you were interested in just stopping by the hotel for a meal, a steak dinner, with pie, would generate a bill of 75-cents.

Yes, you did read that correctly, 75-cents, three-quarters of a dollar.

It was another time.

After dinner, it was the same routine of cleaning the tables, washing the dishes, then preparing the box lunches for the commercial fishermen for the next day before the girls could go to bed.

The Swenson girls, for all their hard work, never received tips, although we should qualify that statement and mention "attempted" tips.

There was one occasion when a traveling salesman (wink, wink) stopped by the hotel and requested a room for the night.

He had been "over served" at one of the local saloons.

Holly, who was older at the time, agreed to take him upstairs and show him an available room.

The traveling salesman said the room looked fine. As he stumbled inside, he offered Holly some "folding money" as a tip.

Holly was so afraid that she took off running down the hallway at a full gallop, leaving the guy with his mouth hanging open in astonishment.

It was rumored that the salesman quit drinking and entered a monastery after the incident, but that was never confirmed.

While we're on the side notes, there was another interesting incident that happened at the Wigwam.

During the summer, Holly's sister, Ruby, would sleep in a screen porch attached to the front of the hotel.

It was cooler, and offered privacy from the rest of the family.

On this particular evening, a guest had talked Maria into renting him the screen porch for the night.

Ruby was on a date with one of the fine young men in Port Wing.

When she returned, she jumped into bed and, thinking it was Holly beside her, said: "Move over."

The individual was more than happy to move over and did so, quickly making room for Ruby.

Ruby soon realized it wasn't Holly, which sent another Swenson girl through the hotel at a full gallop.

When the guest arrived for breakfast the next morning, Ruby said: "Did I scare you?"

The guest's response: "Not at all. I was pleasantly surprised."

The Wigwam Hotel prided itself on developing a family atmosphere.

The rooms were neat and clean, the sheets and pillowcases were ironed each day, the meals were prompt and plentiful, and the staff enjoyed visiting with their guests.

Indeed, it was the family atmosphere that kept guests coming back time after time.

Springtime was especially busy when fishermen from "down south" would descend on Port Wing to take advantage of the prolific fishing on the Flagg River.

At one point, the Orienta dam was under repair and what is now Highway 13 was being constructed.

Crews from both projects stayed at the hotel, but they sat at their own tables and didn't mingle with the other crew.

As a result, the Swenson girls would come into the kitchen and say: "We need more mashed potatoes for that dam table," or "The bridge table is out of carrots."

In 1939, commercial fishermen from Door County, hearing of the fertile fishing grounds on Lake Superior, began arriving in Port Wing.

Some of them stayed for a lifetime.

Refrigeration was a particular problem for a small hotel like the Wigwam in the early years.

Ice was the only method of refrigeration.

Consequently, Robert would spend a good share of the winter cutting large ice cakes from the slough on Lake Bibon and then hauling them, with horses and skidders, to the hotel.

At the hotel, the ice cakes were placed in the icehouse, which was a large storage shed lined with sawdust to keep the ice from melting in the summer heat.

In the summer, ice would be chipped off the cakes and brought into the pantry of the hotel, where they were placed in the "icebox," which kept meat and perishables cool.

When the ice melted, the routine began anew.

Speaking of Robert Swenson, Holly's father, you're probably wondering what his role was in this hotel endeavor, since he hasn't been mentioned much during this story.

Robert had other business ventures that developed income for the Swenson family while Maria and the girls were running the hotel.

He owned a threshing machine and clover hauler.

During the harvest, he would be working the "meatball run" between Cornucopia and Port Wing, helping farmers bring in the crop.

It was named the "meatball run" because a meatball dinner greeted Robert at every stop.

Robert also operated a sawmill for a time.

It was located on Washington Avenue at the site of the first bridge leading down to the marina.

The Wigwam Hotel closed its doors in 1956, when physical problems made it impossible for Maria to continue operating the business.

All the girls were grown.

Marvel was a teacher for some 30 years in Wisconsin and Minnesota.

Marvel met her future husband, Hugh Erickson, while she was teaching in St. Paul.

Marvel and Hugh traveled extensively during their working years and then retired to Florida.

Laverne also got married and raised a family in St. Paul.

Ruby lived in Grand Marais for many years, where she and her husband, Carl Ogren, worked at the electric company, but they eventually moved to St. Paul as well.

Only Holly remained in Port Wing.

She married Robert Carlson, one of those Door County fishermen who stayed in the hotel.

It was a union that lasted 56 years.

The Wigwam Hotel was vacant for several years after the Swenson family closed the doors.

It later was purchased by the Picher family and used as a private home.

Hale O'Malley, from Cornucopia, also owned the Wigwam for a time.

Its current owner is Nora Tribys.

Holly is 82 now, but she's a young woman again when she travels Washington Avenue, with wonderful memories of her family and her years at the Wigwam Hotel in Port Wing, including that bright, spring, day when a young fisherman from Door County, Robert Carlson, arrived at the door.

She's a young girl, skipping across the street to the Lundgren Block for a 5-cent ice cream cone or visiting the Creamery for a chunk of pure, freshly churned, butter.

The memories are there of a once bustling business district, but things have changed a lot in Port Wing over the last 75 years.

The business operations from the 1920's....30's and 40's have disappeared.

One church remains in that capacity.

Two of the other churches have become an art gallery and a pottery shop.

It isn't necessary to cut ice from the slough anymore for summer refrigeration, an ice cream cone is substantially more than 5-cents and a steak dinner is a whole lot more than 75-cents.

All things come to an end at some point, but for the Swenson family and the Wigwam Hotel, it was a good run.

GERT DIAMON

We would expect to find precious stones in the diamond mines of Africa, but we all too often neglect to look for precious gems closer to home, like northern Wisconsin.

A case in point is the Diamon we found in Iron River.

She is Gert Diamon, an absolute "gem" of crystal clarity.

Gert was born, some 81 years ago, at the Grandish home in Herbster, Wisconsin, with the assistance of a mid-wife.

Her family moved to Herbster from Pennsylvania in March of 1922, leaving a house in Ford City, with electricity, to take up residence in a tiny northern Wisconsin town in a home with no electricity.

Gert's sister, Anne, called the move "exciting and exhilarating!"

In Herbster, Gert and her family lived in a neighborhood of families much like their own.

Isaksson's lived across the road and to the south of the Grandish family.

The Kleinhan's farm was behind Isaksson's.

It was enormous, with one house for the owner and another for the family that ran the farm for Mr. Kleinhans.

The Sorenson's lived just across the road.

Gert and her family lived just a smidgen short of a mile from the schoolhouse, so the bus would not pick them up each morning.

Consequently, this is one of those stories where Gert and her brothers and sisters really did walk a mile, each way, to school every day, although Gert admits it wasn't uphill both ways.

Times were hard in northern Wisconsin when Gert was a child, but then, times were hard for everyone.

Wealth was found in family and friendship.

Gert's sister, Marie, left home after the 10th grade and worked for a family in Duluth.

She wasn't allowed to eat with the host family and slept in a lonely room in the attic.

Marie was heartbroken much of the time, but she did graduate from High School in Duluth.

Gert's father, Michael Grandish, believed in education.

Michael thought it was the best thing America had to offer, and he wanted his children to take advantage of every educational opportunity.

Anne and Helen both became registered nurses.

It was Anne who Gert calls "The Guardian Angel" of the family.

Anne sent the family $5 each week from her paycheck.

Why?

"Because that's what sister's are supposed to do."

Gert enjoyed every moment at Herbster school.

She grew up to be honored as the Prom Queen at Herbster High (Bobby Uedelhofen was Prom King that year) and she was the first in the Grandish family to graduate from High School.

Gert was 16 years old.

After two years at the University of Wisconsin/Milwaukee, she was off to the big city, Chicago, and a new adventure.

Her first job was at the W. D. Allen Company at State and Lake in Chicago.

Gert paid $10 a month to sleep on a davenport, but the $10 also included all her meals.

She didn't earn a king's ransom at the job, but she still managed to save money from her paycheck each week.

The vault for her savings was an envelope that she tucked in the bottom of her shoe.

She knew where her savings account was every minute.

The next stop was Iron River, where she worked for a time as a bookkeeper for the American Agriculture Association.

Gert was glad to be back home, in northern Wisconsin.

Then came a letter from Norma Helsing.

Norma was joining the WAVES and wanted to know if Gert would be interested in her job at the Port Wing bank.

Gert accepted, at $12.50 a week, and moved into the Wigwam Hotel, just up the street from the bank.

Gert lived in the Wigwam Hotel, where she also took all her meals, until she got married.

While she worked at the bank, Gert met Dan and Ione Daley.

They forged a very close relationship and to this day she considers Dan and Ione to be a part of her own family.

Soon after taking the job in Port Wing, Gert bought her first car, a two-door coupe from the estate of Fred Hillmer, for $188.

Kowabunga!!!!

How 'bout that for a deal?

In the 1940's, weekend entertainment in the summer centered on town league baseball.

This particular Sunday afternoon, Gert was introduced to a young outfielder in Iron River by the name of Chuck Diamon.

A spark was generated.

Chuck was an Iron River boy, the son of Charles and Charlotte Diamon.

As Gert tells it, Chuck truly was a depression baby.

Every cent counted during those difficult years.

Gert recalls Chuck's mother giving him a quarter, then sending him to Herman and Johnson's grocery store for two pounds of hamburger.

On the way out the door, she would yell: "Don't forget the change!"

Are you kiddin' me?

Two pounds of hamburger and change for a quarter?

Hubba…Hubba!!

Chuck and Gert were married on May 4, 1946, at St. Francis Xavier church in Herbster.

It was an exciting day.

As Gert entered the church, her eyes were on Chuck.

Walking down the aisle, she kept repeating: "There he is, daddy….. there he is!!!!"

Love is a simple language, but it speaks volumes.

Chuck was a police officer for many years, so the two of them became quite accustomed to his being called out after they had retired for the night.

Frequently, Chuck would return home, crawl into bed and hear Gert whisper: "Anybody I know?"

Chuck's standard reply: "Who do you know?"

Gert and Chuck were best friends for some 40 years.

What a wonderful legacy!

After they were married, Gert and Chuck saved enough money to buy an 80-acre farm from Robert and Ruth Hooper on Highway A, six miles north of Iron River.

They bought the farm for $3000, with $1000 down and payments of $1000 per year on the balance.

Life was sweet, for a short time, but they soon realized that, no matter how hard they tried, they could not afford to live on the farm.

That didn't translate into giving up, that was not a part of their vocabulary, it just meant they had to identify a solution to the problem.

The solution came quickly.

Chuck went to work in the cold and ice of Greenland, where he helped in the construction of an airport.

He was gone four months.

When he returned, they paid off the farm.

Strength of character, it always perseveres.

It has been an interesting life for Gert, a life that has had the ups and downs we all face.

She has faced each of these situations with dignity and courage.

Chuck died in 1986, after a marriage that produced three sons.

Michael is the oldest, at 58.

He served our Country for 23 years as an Air Force officer, retiring as a Lieutenant Colonel before setting up permanent housekeeping with his wife, Mary Delle, and their three children in Niceville (That's right, it's not a misprint...Niceville), in the Florida panhandle.

Michael is currently a consultant for the U.S. Government.

David is next in line, he's 47.

He lives in Ione, California with his wife, Jennifer, and their two children.

The youngest son, 45-year-old Dan, is well-known in northern Wisconsin as a Certified Paramedic, working with the Gold Cross Ambulance Service.

He has been instrumental in the lives of many northern Wisconsin and Minnesota residents over the past few decades through his paramedic duties.

Dan lives in Poplar, Wisconsin, with his wife, Camille, and their three children.

Gert positively glows when she speaks of her three sons.

These days, when Gert thinks back to her days growing up in Herbster, she is filled with a warmth that everyone always felt when they entered her childhood home.

She and Chuck worked hard to develop the same warmth in their home....and succeeded.

Gert still loves the "Big Water," Lake Superior.

She thinks back to days on the beach, a roaring fire in the evening, hot dogs roasted over an open fire......

And then there were the dances.

Ah.....the dances.

Gert's mother thought the Cornie boys were a little mature for her and her sisters, but she thought they could dance with the Herbster and Port Wing boys as much as they wanted.

They did.

Gert has always been strong in the Catholic faith, a strength that continues today.

It provides her with a spiritual foundation.

The kind heart of this soft-spoken woman is evident in a first conversation.

I particularly admire the tremendous respect and admiration Gert still shows for her mother and father, even after all these years.

Her depth of love is inspiring, as is this anecdote.

When Gert was a child, her mother let it slip that she had never had a doll when she was growing up.

Gert filed that away for future reference.

When Gert grew up, she bought her mother a doll and presented it to her.

It became one of her mother's most cherished possessions.

"Honor thy Father and Mother."

That sounds familiar.

Gert's reverent definition of Herbster, her home town, is reflective of the life most of us search for every day.

> "It is a place where we worked and expected nothing in return, because we were so comfortable with our life."

Wow!

How many times have you heard that in today's society?

When her children and grandchildren showed a continuing interest in the family history, Gert felt the information should be cataloged and passed on to coming generations.

As a result, this remarkable and sensitive woman has put together a wonderful series of stories that outline her life, complete with pictures.

Gert tells me she authored the family history to make a point… "You don't need a lot to be happy."

Most of the information in this story comes from that chronicle.

It is inspirational.

It is fascinating.
It is heartwarming.
It is thought provoking.
It is entitled: "Thank You For Asking."
Gert Diamon…..a "gem" in northern Wisconsin.
We're glad we asked!

Live Every Day Like It's Your Last Day!

-- Author Unknown

THE PRETTY PONY

I'd like to tell you a story about a kid who grew up in Minnesota.

The kid had just managed to get his drivers license and had his sights set on owning his own car.

The next challenge was putting together enough cash to buy a car, any car.

Back then, more than 40 years ago, the best bet to earn enough money to buy a car was to work during the summer, baling hay and cleaning barns for the local farmers.

He didn't make enough to buy a car that first summer, but he was back again the next summer, and the summer after that, eating dust behind the baler and scratching his itching back raw when the loose hay was drawn to his sweating body, like a magnet, during those scorching summer days.

Didn't matter ... had to have that car.

The magic day finally arrived.

He scraped together enough money to buy a sweet little Mustang convertible, ebony black, white top, red interior, four-speed.

From that point on, he spent all his money on things that would make that pony look good on the outside.

New tires, new rims, new paint job, special chrome around the headlights.

Every extra dime this kid could scrape together he put into the glamour items.

At one point, he even had the car jacked up and the rear axle painted.

He would have his buddy drive the Mustang, then he would drive behind the pony in his buddy's car so he could see how cool that painted rear axle looked in the headlights.

If they had had vanity plates at the time, his would have said: "M KOOL."

Another day in the field brought a few more bucks to buy new chrome mirrors.

It went on and on.

No expense spared to make the pony look pretty.

The Mustang had a sweet little 289 under the hood, with a stick shift on the floor, so it could snap up most of the local boys.

Every now and again, if he thought about it, the kid would change the oil or put in a new filter.

It wasn't very often.

He was too cool for that, dragging main with the top down, dropping down a gear so the chicks could hear those new, glass pack, mufflers rumble.

Yeah baby!

Every now and then, the engine would miss, but he didn't have time to change spark plugs.

He was too cool.

Besides, he was tall hog at the trough, wasn't anybody in town could outrun the pony.

Late one summer, a nerdy kid and his family moved into town.

The new kid didn't make an effort to meet the local guys.

Most of the time, he could be found under the hood of his car, a beat up old pea green Pinto.

The locals would laugh as they drove by his house.

He was always working on that pea green Pinto, but no one had ever seen it actually move off his driveway.

Late that summer, just before school started, all of the locals were gathered at the drive-in, talking smart, lookin' cool, checkin' out the chicks.

Some of the boys looked up and saw the new kid coasting.....coasting.... into the drive-in.

Assuming the new kid had run out of gas, the laughing and cat calls began in earnest.

"Hey, ain't you embarrassed to drive that pile of junk?"

"Hey kid, when the needle is on 'E' … it means empty."

The new kid didn't say a word.

He coasted to a stop beside the pretty pony and turned off the lights, waiting patiently for the car hop.

The local kid in the Mustang thought he'd join in the fun.

He looked at the new kid, smirked at the pea green Pinto and said: "I hear ya been doin' a lotta work on that car. Wanna race?"

"Yeah, I guess I could," comes the reply from the new kid.

Smelling another victory for the Mustang, the local kid started his pony and said: "Follow me."

There was a special spot in this small town where the locals went to burn rubber and challenge each other for the fastest car.

The pretty pony always ran in front.

The two horses, the sleek Mustang and the beat up little Pinto, lined up side by side.

The local kid looked over and smirked at the new kid in the pea green Pinto.

The new kid looked straight ahead.

One of the chicks yelled: "GO!"

That pea green Pinto came roaring to life, reared up like a thoroughbred stallion, and was 30 feet down the road before the pretty pony got off the line.

The Pinto was at a full gallop and took out the pretty pony by ten car lengths.

This time the Mustang coasted to a stop.

The new kid was waiting, legs crossed, arms folded, leaning back on the hood of the Pinto.

"Wow!"

It was the only word that matched the performance.

"What have you got in that thing?"

This time it was the new kid's turn to smirk.

He opened up the hood.

The engine, complete with chrome head covers, chrome air filter, and nasty looking attachments, looked like something you would find under the shell of a top fuel funny car.

The horsepower contained under the hood of that ugly old Pinto must have been three times that of the pretty pony.

Inside, the new kid had installed a special shifting package and the dash was alive with all the latest gadgets to measure performance.

"Ya know, I've never been beat," said the local kid.

"Me neither," comes the reply from the new kid.

The local kid learned a good lesson that day.

It's not all that important how you look on the outside.

It's what you have on the inside that's important.

Keep that in mind as you journey through life.

NEVER…NEVER…NEVER GIVE UP!

Some days life just seems to be overwhelming, doesn't it?

The mortgage is due, the kids college tuition is due, there's a car payment coming up, one son has bad grades, a daughter has way too much attitude and the boss doesn't realize you have a life beyond work.

The business person is wondering how to make payroll this week and a grandmother is trying to budget for her prescriptions, while grampa is worried about his doctor appointment next week.

The high school student worries about being popular and the college student worries about life after graduation.

The rich man worries about getting another quarter-percent on his money, while the poor man worries about having any money at all.

No matter who you are, it just seems overwhelming at times.

To quote Thoreau: "The mass of men lead lives of quiet desperation."

It has been this way for hundreds of years, we all have problems, no matter our station in life.

The key to living a happy life is to find the inspiration to hang in there on those days, or weeks, or months, or even years, when the deck seems to be stacked against you.

I remember those years well, when mortgage interests were high and we had three daughters in college, all at the same time.

It seemed we would never have an extra dime.

I learned those many years ago to take inspiration from, of all places, the writing of Shakespeare.

More precisely, from a play Shakespeare wrote in the year 1599, centered on the battle of Agincourt, on the 25th of October, 1415.

The English were outnumbered five to one by the French.

The morale of the English troops was at rock bottom when Henry the Fifth stood before his officers and men to prepare them for battle.

The play is Henry V.

The address from the King comes in Act 4…Scene 3.

"This day is called the feast of Crispian:
He that outlives this day, and comes safe home,
Will stand a tip-toe when the day is named,
And rouse him at the name of Crispian,
He that shall live this day, and see old age,

> Will yearly on the vigil feast his neighbours,
> And say 'To-morrow is Saint Crispian:'
> Then will he strip his sleeve and show his scars.
> And say 'These wounds I had on Crispin's day.'
> Old men forget: yet all shall be forgot,
> But he'll remember with advantages
> What feats he did that day: then shall our names.
> Familiar in the mouth as household words
> Harry the King, Bedford and Exeter,
> Warwick and Talbot, Salisbury and Gloucester,
> Be in their flowing cups freshly remember'd.
> This story shall the good man teach his son;
> And Crispin Crispian shall ne'er go by,
> From this day to the ending of the world,
> But we in it shall be remember'd;
> We few, we happy few, we band of brothers;
> For he to-day that sheds his blood with me
> Shall be my brother; be he ne'er so vile,
> This day shall gentle his condition:
> And gentlemen in England now a-bed
> Shall think themselves accursed they were not here,
> And hold their manhoods cheap whiles any speaks
> That fought with us on Saint Crispin's day."

To this day, I'm choked with emotion each time I read the speech of Henry V.

For me, the Battle of Agincourt is everyday life.

I have read the speech countless times over the past 20 years, frequently when I was about to take on great risk and challenge, when I questioned myself, when my confidence wavered.

It inspires me.

It calms me.

It makes me believe I can accomplish anything!

It speaks to me of accepting life's challenges.

It speaks to me of continuing to move forward against overwhelming odds.

It speaks to me of holding others close to you and sharing the pride of completing a seemingly impossible task, sometimes a task as simple as meeting the mortgage payment for the month or buying groceries for the week.

It reminds me to never, ever, give up.

There are moments in our lives when we have all felt helpless and outnumbered, when the pressures of life and work have pushed us to the edge.

You may be fighting the battle now.

Don't give up!

I have been there, I have stood on the ridge and listened to King Henry before the Battle of Agincourt, I have lived through that day to see old age and now strip my sleeve to show my scars and say: "These wounds I had on Crispin's Day."

We all have wounds from life.

Don't give up!

We all face challenges that seem insurmountable.

Don't give up!

We all want to find safe haven, to back away from taking chances in life, to find the safe harbor, but sometimes we have to swim in deep water and cross high bridges, even if we're afraid.

Don't be afraid to be afraid …you're the only one who knows.

I have been there many times.

Don't give up!

Another Englishman, Winston Churchill, spoke of tenacity and courage in a speech at Harrow School on October 29, 1941.

It was a time of World War II, the British had been pounded mercilessly by the Germans, but held on to fight back and turn the tide in their favor.

These are quotes from his closing remarks that day.

"Never give in. Never give in. Never, never, never, never…in nothing, great or small, large or petty…never give in, except to convictions of honor and good sense.

Never yield to force.

Never yield to the apparently overwhelming might of the enemy."

The British didn't yield, and they don't speak German.

Don't give up!

Life ain't easy.

It is a series of moments, interspersed with great joy and paralyzing pain, with opportunity and challenge, with failure and success.

All in all, it is what you make it.

Stare down the challenges, swim in the deep water, walk across the high bridges, and most importantly……

Don't give up!

By the way, Henry V and his troops, outnumbered five to one by the French, won the Battle of Agincourt in 1415.

Don't give up!

Don't worry about Yesterday!
Do what needs to be done today!
Tomorrow will take care of itself.

-- Author Unknown

THE EULOGY

Some time ago, a good friend of mine and I decided that the survivor will deliver a eulogy at the others funeral.

It wasn't until recently, when I developed some health problems and realized we are both getting older, that I began to give some thought to what I would say if I'm the person at the podium.

When our journey ends, there will be, for most of us, a granite marker with two dates chiseled in the stone.

There's no guarantee how much time will be reflected on that piece of granite showing the beginning and the end of our life, and I guess it isn't all that important.

What is important is what transpired between the dates.

Did we make a difference?

If I am the speaker, I won't be spending time talking about the cars my friend drove or the houses he built.

I won't be spending time on the stock he bought or the money he had in the bank when his clock expired.

I won't be spending time on rings and jewelry or vacations to exotic locations.

I won't be talking about the athletic honors he earned or the plaques he had to commemorate his many corporate accomplishments.

These aren't the important things between the dates.

We all spend too much time on the things we have and the things we want.

In the end, we haven't spent enough time on the things that matter.

What does matter, in that time between the dates, is the difference we have made.

I will be able to say that my friend made a difference.

I will talk about the many people he mentored and helped up the ladder of success.

I will speak of the genuine concern he had for the feelings of others and how his gruff outer shell cloaked a person of deep emotion.

I will talk about the choice he made to leave the rat race and enter the human race.

That decision allowed him to trade money for time and power for purpose.

That decision allowed him, in his 50th year, to go fishing on Wednesdays and spend quiet Friday afternoons over a long lunch with his wife.

So, if I am the person at the podium, I will speak of those quiet times, about the innermost feelings he shared, sitting in a boat early on a Wednesday morning.

I will speak of the tears that unexpectedly appeared during one of those Friday afternoon lunches with his wife.

He blamed the tears on allergies.

The laugh lines around her eyes crinkled when she smiled at him.

He laughed as well.

They both knew it wasn't allergies.

I will speak of phone calls on Tuesday and pizza on Thursday.

I will speak of Friday fish fry's and deer hunting in November.

I will speak of antique malls and coffee shops.

I will tell his children how proud he was to be their father.

I will remind his wife, his best friend, how often he said: "You are everything I wish I could be."

On that day he re-entered the human race, he never wanted to be away from her again, even for a day.

I will talk about all the good things I remember about my good friend.

When I do this, I will look at his friends and see tears, because they know I am speaking of a man who made a difference in his time between the dates.

At the end of my friends eulogy, I shall say:

"My dad told me when I was very young that I would have a successful life if, at the end, I had five friends I could count on to be there for me, no matter what the circumstance.

I only have four left.

We will miss your wit and charm, we will miss your smile and laugh, but, most importantly, we will miss you.

Fair winds and trailing seas on your new journey, my friend.

I love ya, man."

So…my friend and me…we are beginning to feel our mortality.

We are both wondering who will be at the podium.

As we get older, we begin to think about these things…we begin to question whether we have made a difference.

I've not given nearly enough thought to what will be said if I am not the person at the podium, but I hope I would be proud of what my friend would have to say about my time between the dates.

25 IN A ROW

Laurie and I were fortunate enough to celebrate our 25th Anniversary recently.

It's passed in the blink of an eye.

I wish I could say it has been a fairy tale romance over the past quarter century, but that would not be the truth.

Like all couples who have been together a long time, we rode the roller coaster of emotion over the years.

Sometimes the ride is thrilling, sometimes you just have to hang on tight to keep from throwing up.

We have faced the same fears, the same frustrations, as any couple, but throughout we have always been each others best friend.

Through cheers, fears, tears, and triumph, that has never changed.

I think our friendship has been the critical factor in keeping us together through the difficult times.

The wedding vows say: "till death do us part,"….not: "until it is no longer convenient."

We have respected those vows, and each other, for a quarter century.

If that isn't modern day thinking, I guess we're pretty happy to be a part of the old school.

It's a special time, that 25th Anniversary, so I thought it would be better to write my own card for the occasion, rather than buy one at the card shop.

At the risk of appearing sappy, I'd like to share with you what I have to say to Laurie on this special day:

Twenty five years ago, the sunshine came back into my life when I married you.

You've been my best friend all these years.

You've shown me, a crusty old character, that the more love you give, the more you get.

Your children, and me, feel privileged to have you as a part of our lives.

Your gentle soul has calmed the waters of our family storms over these many years.

Twenty five years ago, I wanted to impress you with dollars and diamonds.

We had little of either back then, and the importance of both has diminished over the years.

Wealth is measured differently as we get older.

A quarter century later, you are the only diamond I need in my life and there aren't enough dollars in the world to purchase the love and respect I have for you.

I love you more today than yesterday, but less than tomorrow, and when my final hours are down to a few, my final thoughts will be of you.

Happy Anniversary!

I'm a lucky man!

Twenty five years ago, Cinderella stepped out of her carriage and found a frog along the road.

She knew the drill.

If she kissed the frog, it would turn into a handsome Prince.

She did kiss the frog, but there was no magic Prince after the kiss, just a frog, wasn't even a handsome frog.

Cinderella kept the frog anyway, and for that I will be eternally grateful.

Cinderella is still kissing the frog.

Still no handsome Prince.

Just that old frog.

Hope springs eternal.

Friends are not a dime a dozen.
They are priceless!

G.D. Perkins

GOING HOME

I have been privileged over the years to have been invited to be a featured speaker at various events.

That hasn't been a part of my life for several years now, but I was always honored when a group allowed me to be a part of their day.

Just this afternoon, I came across an address I gave to a group in Arizona, more than five years ago.

It was the last time I spoke in front of a group.

If I may, I would like to share an edited version of those Arizona thoughts with you.

I must tell you that I'm not here this morning to be a teacher.

I can't tell you where to find more prospects or make more sales.

I can't tell you how to make more money.

I'm a storyteller.

I talk about life…because I believe it is to be lived 24 hours a day…. every day.

I talk about talent…because I believe we have a duty to use all we have.

I talk about making a difference…because we can.

Today is the greatest day of my life…and it is the greatest day of your life as well.

If you don't believe every day is the greatest day of your life…try missing one.

It's all perspective…isn't it?

That's what life is all about…perspective.

It's how you see it.

Life is a do it to yourself project.

You can have a good day, or you can have a bad day.

You make the call…you take the responsibility.

Get rid of the…..coulda'…shoulda'…woulda'…mighta'…"if only ida" and "I wish ida."

Replace them with ….."I can"…"I will" … "I did."

Life is one-percent what happens to you and 99-percent how you react to it.

Unfortunately, we've become a nation of victims, where no one is willing to accept personal responsibility for their actions.

The operative statement of the day in far too many instances is: "Not my fault!"

Instead of fixing the blame....let's fix the problem.

The greatest mistake we can make in life is to be constantly afraid of making a mistake.

Have a bad day?

So what?

Get over it.

The darkest hour is still only sixty minutes long.

I must have been eight or nine years old when my dad took me to the back door of a meat market in our home town.

The butcher came out and gave him a box of meat scraps, which became our evening meal.

Yes...we were poor and needed help at that particular time.

Times were tough for our family.

There are those who would pity my dad for taking the scraps, but I have a different perspective.

My dad fixed a problem that night.

He did what he had to do.

We survived.

I never forgot that night.

The most important thing I learned is that one person can make a difference.

Don't fix the blame...fix the problem.

A hundred years from now...it won't matter what your bank account was or what kind of house you lived in or what kind of car you drove, but if you've made a difference in someone's life, it will be reflected and passed on to the next generation.

I hope I've done that during my lifetime...that I've made a difference in someone's life...because I remember a man who made a difference in mine.

He was the owner of a meat market, in a small town in western Minnesota.

I don't know if Spike Splitoster was a rich man or a poor man, but I remember his act of kindness more than a half-century ago.

We remember those who have a positive impact on our lives.

The people who make a difference in our lives are not the ones with the most money or the impressive credentials.

They are the people who care about you...truly care about you.

If you were accused of making a difference, would you be guilty?

We live in unique times.

Today we have higher buildings and wider highways…but shorter tempers and a more narrow view of life.

We spend more….we enjoy less.

These are times of breathtaking houses…but more broken homes.

We went to the moon and back…but we don't cross the street to talk to our neighbors.

We talk a lot…we love way too little and we hate way too much.

I guess Ozzie and Harriet have moved….somewhere.

Have we lost the innocence and joy of living that we had back in the 1950's?

We have become a cynical people.

Let's replace that cynicism with optimism…the biology of hope.

Every day that you live is a special occasion, so you don't need to keep anything for that………special occasion.

Read more books…sit on the porch and hold hands with someone you love.

Let's write that letter we were going to get to………. "one of these days."

Tell your family how much you love them and never pass up the chance to laugh at yourself.

Every day….every hour…every minute…every second is special… because you don't know if it will be your last.

Life is a picnic.

Don't leave any crumbs.

I'll be going home for Christmas in a few days.

Home is a little village on the shore of Lake Superior, in northern Wisconsin.

It's a Swedish community, settled by fishermen and loggers more than a century ago.

The village of Port Wing.

I'm privileged to be a part of the community.

If you relax and close your eyes for a few moments, I'd like to show you around town.

Highway 13 goes right through the middle of the village.

Most of the coffee club show up at the Cottage Café, promptly at six o'clock every morning.

The coffee is always on.

Smoky's store opens a little later in the morning.

The pottery shop and the art gallery are closed for the winter.

If you look off to the north, you can see the big water, Lake Superior.

Even in the winter, it's beautiful.

The Town Hall is just across the street from Smokey's store, and if you look across the park to the west, you can see the museum and the fire hall.

The South Shore and Port Bar are just up the road on Highway 13.

Washington Avenue wanders down toward the lake.

The Lutheran church is off to the left.

We just dedicated the new elevator a few weeks ago.

That sure helps the folks who struggle to get up the stairs.

Several times a year, we watch the northern lights dancing through the night sky.

The beach at the marina is the best spot to watch these celestial shows.

Sometimes they're so beautiful they bring tears to my eyes.

We live on Washington Avenue.

Barney and Dorrie live next door.

The post office is just up the block.

I always enjoy visiting with Jeff, the postmaster.

He brings me up to date on the bear and deer season.

The bank is across the street from the post office.

Claudette and Laverne have been there a long time.

Laverne just finished preparations for the Swedish meatball feed.

He's always in charge of the mashed potatoes.

Tells me the recipe every year....half a cup of sugar with the butter.... that's the secret.

Laverne always asks me: "When ya coming home for good?"

My answer is always the same: "Pretty soon now."

It's Christmas....so Laurie has the smell of cookies in the house.

I love that smell.

You know, it always occurs to me, at some point when I'm home, that I'm part of a Norman Rockwell painting.

I'm living in Ozzie and Harriet's town.

Those days, long past, are still alive here in our town.

Port Wing is a great place to live.

If you're passing through, stop and see us.

We're the white house with the picket fence, next to Barney and Dorrie.

The coffee will be on and we'll have a chance to discuss a few of life's questions.

Where are you?
How long have you been there?
Most importantly…..where are you going?

I know where I'm going.
I'm going home.
Merry Christmas!

So, that's an edited version of the last time I had a chance to brag about Port Wing before an audience.

There have been a few changes in our village over the past five years, but most things have remained the same.

I'm lucky enough to be home for good now.

Connie has joined Claudette and Laverne at the bank.

The Cottage Café has been sold and there's a new owner at the Port Bar.

Smoke still runs the store.

The pottery shop and the art gallery are doing well.

Sharon opened up another gallery and ice cream shop on Washington Avenue a few years ago.

Chet and Jeanette are now our neighbors to the south.

Barney and Dorrie are still our neighbors to the north.

Couple of the private wells have gone dry because of a few dry summers in a row, but it's still Port Wing.

We adjust to the changes.

We look out for each other.

Ozzie and Harriet still live here.

It's good to be home.

"You will not go through
life undefeated."

-- Don Imus

THE FINAL WORD

So….you have read the final dispatch that has come to you via "Rural Delivery."

I hope you've enjoyed the mail.

In this brief journey, we have reflected on happy times and sad times, on tough times and touching times, all part of our journey through life.

All moments suspended in time that frame the patchwork of a lifetime.

In the final analysis, we will get out of life what we put into it.

We have choices.

There's a lot of traffic on the easy road, but there's a reason for that, IT'S THE EASY ROAD!

Everyone wants to travel on that highway.

The extraordinary person, irrespective of their background, irrespective of problems, or poverty, or humble beginnings, will take the Hard Road Highway, filled with rocks and ravines, challenges at every turn, and a speed bump every few miles.

There's no guarantee what you'll find on this road, other than an opportunity to continue on down the line….. if you're strong enough to go the extra mile.

We have choices.

We can be a leader or a loser.

We have choices.

We can be a winner or a whiner.

We have choices.

Those who complain about the cards they've been dealt spend all of their time looking for a new deal.

There are four aces in every deck.

Play the hand you have!

We have choices.

Several years ago, I was within a few hours of dying.

I heard a doctor say: "His pressure is 60 over 40….we're losing him!"

It was the second time in my life that I experienced a life changing event.

From that point forward, I have never had a bad day.

We have choices.

When people ask me: "How's it goin'?"..... my standard response is: "Today is the greatest day of my life!"

More often than not, I receive a less than enthusiastic response.

I feel badly for those people who don't see rainbow's through the rain.

After my life changing experience, every day is a bonus, every day is indeed, "the greatest day of my life."

If you don't believe that every day is the greatest day of YOUR life, try missing one day.

It's all attitude.

For me......every day is Saturday and every meal is a banquet.

I'm often accused of being a Pollyanna because my attitude is always up and positive.

More often than not...those individuals also throw in the phrase: "You don't know what it's like to face tough times."

Yes...I do.

I've been on the wrong side of the tracks.

I remember opening the refrigerator to find nothing but three pieces of bread and a jar of mustard.

I remember going to the back door of that butcher shop with my dad.

I remember choices of food or fuel.

I'm still here.

There aren't many people in the world who were born with a silver spoon in their mouth and a trust account in the bank.

A good many of us come from the wrong side of the tracks, but that doesn't mean we can't get on the train.

We live in America!

There is opportunity.....look for it!

We have all, every one of us, faced tough times during the course of a lifetime, but as Dr. Robert Schuller says: "Tough times don't last....tough people do."

Whatever problem you're facing today, choose to stare it down, choose to reach down for a strength you never thought you had......choose to make your life better.

I alluded earlier to experiencing the second life changing event in my life.

Here's the first.

More than three decades ago, I made a choice that has impacted every day of my life since.

I am an alcoholic.

That fact is not something I'm proud of, but, by the same token, I'm not ashamed of it either.

It is what it is.

It's been more than thirty years since I've had a drink, but that doesn't change what I am......I am an alcoholic.

I didn't become an alcoholic because my parents treated me badly as a child.

They didn't.

I didn't become an alcoholic because of a tragic event in my life.

I didn't become an alcoholic because someone hurt my feelings when I was six years old.

I became an alcoholic because I chose to drink a lot.....and I liked it.

I also chose to stop drinking.

I'm not a crusader for the reinstatement of prohibition.

Some people can handle alcohol....I can't.

It took a long time for me to come to that realization, but if I hadn't, my life would have ended years ago.

We all make a decision at some point in our life to give up or get up.

I chose the latter of the two.

Yesterday is yesterday, we can't change it, let it go........get over it.

Today is another day of opportunity.

The bottom line is this.....we can choose to spend our days on top of the world....or we can choose to spend our days with the world on top of us.

We have choices.

Carpe Diem.

"Life is a picnic…
Don't leave crumbs."

G.D. Perkins

Printed in the United States
127016LV00004B/1/P